WHO OWNS YOU?
THE MONSTERS OF MIDGARD

DOMINA EASTON

DARK WOODS PUBLISHING

CONTENTS

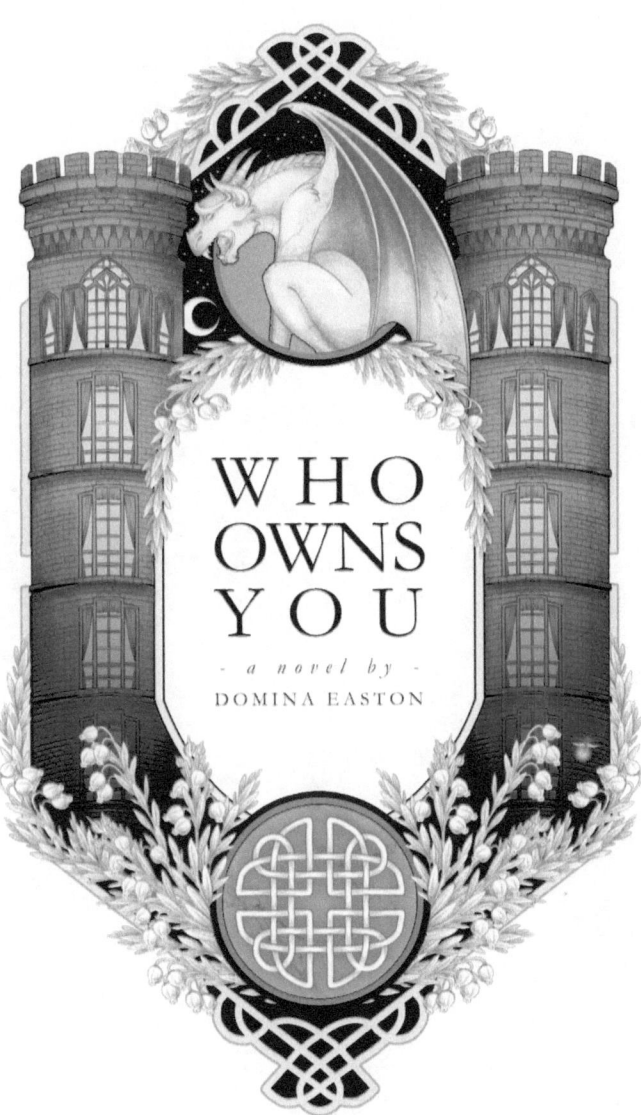

WHO
OWNS
YOU

- *a novel by* -

DOMINA EASTON

For my those who feel the vibes are paramount in the smutty stories they read.

CONTENT WARNINGS

Magic going haywire/causing harm, puke, FMC
experiencing fatphobia (past), some struggles with self confidence,
mentions of parental death (past), MMC getting majorly injured,
heavy sexual content, soulmates/bonds that are fought against,
light bullying, irresponsible actions, implications of past abuse,
abuse by a parental figure toward MMC (past, not shown).

If any of these would cause you discomfort please put yourself first.

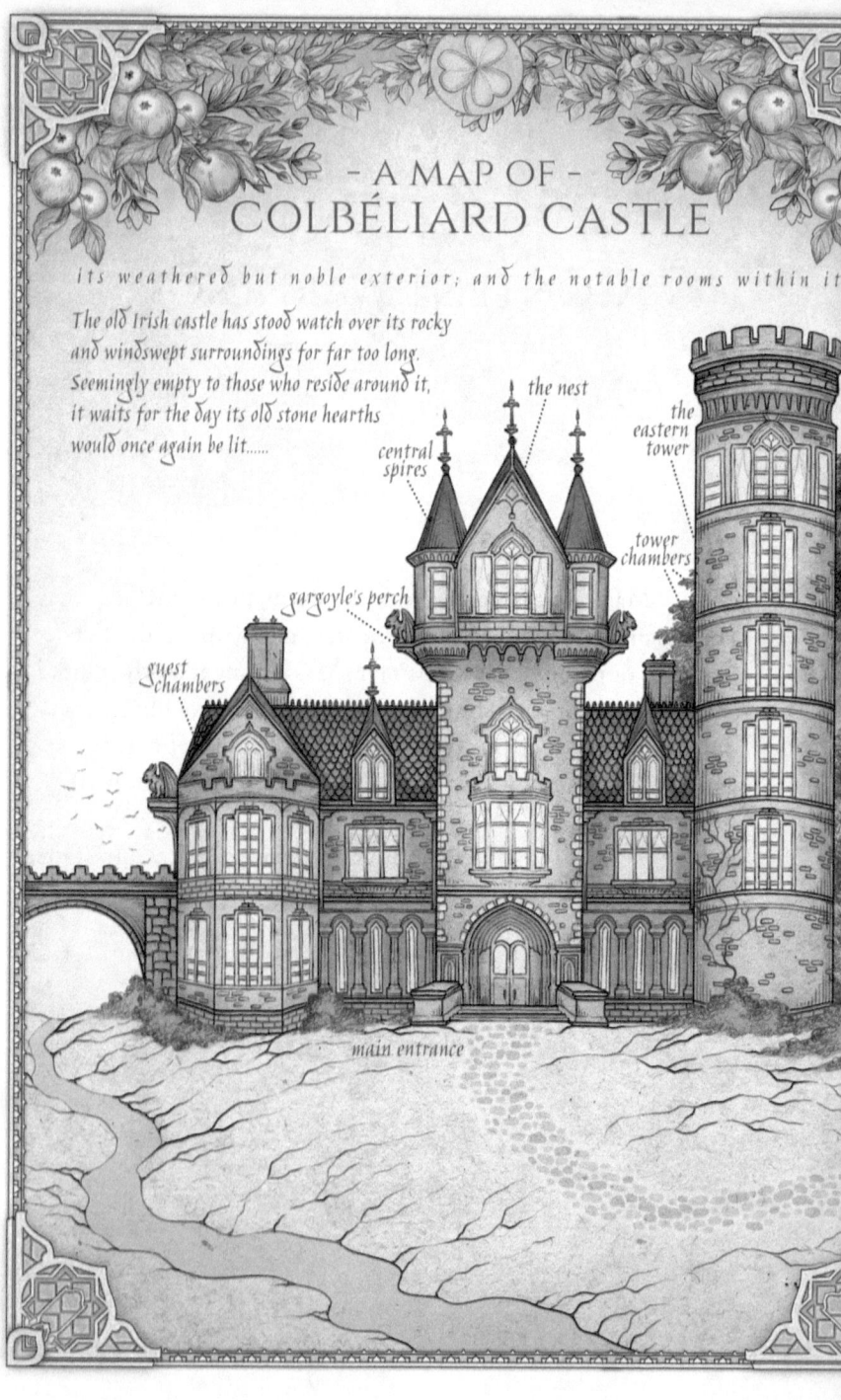

– A MAP OF –
COLBÉLIARD CASTLE

its weathered but noble exterior; and the notable rooms within it

The old Irish castle has stood watch over its rocky
and windswept surroundings for far too long.
Seemingly empty to those who reside around it,
it waits for the day its old stone hearths
would once again be lit......

the nest

the
eastern
tower

central
spires

tower
chambers

gargoyle's perch

guest
chambers

main entrance

central spires

the eastern tower

tower watchroom

guest quarters

gargoyle's perch

tower chambers

the nest

Marcus' room

guest chambers

Julius' room

Darius' room

Charlotte's room

common room

the bridge

the study

Atlas' room

bath room

the studio

art storage

the kitchen, top floor

the great chamber

to the basement

the kitchen, bottom floor

cold cellars

the great ascent

PROLOGUE

ATLAS

THOU SHALT NOT SUFFER a witch stealing your fucking house. Especially when said house is the ancestral castle of your nest's alpha. My eyes find the bastard in question. Darius is tapping away on his laptop like his home isn't under threat by an unknown witch. The white glow of his screen makes the powdery blue of his stone look bleached, like it's been left in the sun too long. His stupid face is also far too calm. Like we haven't been in this attic for over a day already and will be for an indeterminate amount of time. It's a good thing we don't *need* food or water or to use the bathroom. The small luxuries of living aren't necessities when you're made of stone and magic.

Born or forged, gargoyles are the same once they take their first breath, even if those who are born don't see it that way. A bitter taste coats my tongue, and my eyes fall on our alpha and then my other nest-mates. They've never known about the disdainful looks, the whispered jabs, and outright vile threats against my *tainted stone* directed at me when we meet with the other world protector gargoyles, and I'll never let them know. It would only make them

1

more unbearably protective of me. Youngest and the troublemaker forever, I suppose.

Scoffing, I cast my gaze over to our alpha.

"What?" he asks, crossing one leg clad in black slacks over the other like this dusty attic is the most lavish room in the castle.

The way he acts makes my magic boil in my veins. All the humor I felt a moment ago freezes into distaste. *How can he be so blasé about all this?*

"How the hell can you stand it?" I ask, barely keeping the hiss out of my words.

"Stand what? Your attitude?" He smirks, and I force my eyes not to roll.

"Har, har. No, you arsehole. Letting a strange witch do as she pleases with our home."

"And what exactly do you think she's doing? Hexing every corner and hall?" The chuckle he barely tries to hide pisses me off further.

I roll my shoulders, trying to keep my hands loose. It's not good to get into fights with your nest-mates, but for the last few days, I've been more on edge than I have in centuries.

"I don't care what she's doing or not doing. It's not about—" I scoff and run my hand through my hair, pushing the dark, dusky strands from my face. "It's not about the witch." I hiss the word like an insult. "I want to enjoy my space, I want to watch Julius fuck about in the kitchen, I want to see you shit a brick when Marcus breaks another of your precious ancient vases that is ugly as fuck, or whatever he does to piss you off."

"So you're being a brat because you miss your room?" Darius asks, crossing his arms over his chest. All folded up like a pissed-off alpha gargoyle pretzel.

"If that's what you want to call it, then yes, I want my fucking room. I want to wander the house that we have kept safe and sound for hundreds of years. I don't want to act like a fucking dormouse in my home!" I snap, the magic simmering inside me fizzling to the surface.

I feel Darius grab hold of it through the bond and drag it just out of my reach. An alpha's control over the magic of their nest-mates is almost complete. The prick often pulls mine from me.

Of course, I can't even lash out with my own magic.

I tip my head and my neck cracks loudly. If I had been human, I would be dead, but I was never human and would never be.

"Calm yourself, Atlas. I'm going to send a message to Eloise. Once the witch is settled in, we'll have an introduction made. You are right in the respect that we shouldn't have to hide in our home, but you are wrong in the fact that the witch doesn't belong here at all. You know what this old place can be like," he says with a dismissive wave of his hand.

I hiss and fight the urge to punch into the brickwork next to me. The older the building, the more strongly it's connected to the magic of the land it's built on. And Colbéliard is one hell of a magical place.

I bite my lip against further argument as Darius pulls out his slim cell phone and begins to tap away at a text to the only other supernatural we have regular contact with.

The only thing keeping me a little sane is the fact he hasn't caught on that I've turned off the electricity in the main castle or the fact that I've stashed all the towels and extra bedding in this dusty hellhole with us. It is stupidly pleasing. The alpha of my nest is anal when it comes to communication and has backups for his backups, so I knew there was no risk of his devices losing connection.

Though Colbéliard is incredibly magical, the town is small. Before, if there were more than just the handful of us, the humans would notice things were not quite right. Everything is changing, and it's not just the witch that feels wrong. Gargoyles are supposed to be the silent protectors of balance between humans and super-naturals. We are seen in the day but never questioned simply as a part of the architecture. All of that has gone to shit now. Even up in this attic, we know word has gotten out. We have been anticipating it ever since the first whispers of displeasure have rippled through the community.

It's a silly little game of life and fate that some other supernaturals have chosen to play. With long lives, wealth, beauty, and power, there is little a supernatural does not feel they deserve in the world of mortals, and that means that they will need a lot more protection. It forced my nest-mates to quietly try and get ready for how the world would change. My nest-mates and I provide that protection, even if we aren't so visible in the light of day.

"There, done," Darius says, lifting his voice to catch the attention of our nest-mates.

"Where, what?" Marcus asks, eyes flicking about the room like he's looking for a ball or a squirrel.

The poor guy is so understimulated in the attic he's losing his mind. Julius shakes his head, giving a slight wince at Marcus' puppy-like energy before pulling the other man into his side.

Darius's eye twitches, but he brushes over what Marcus said and points at me.

"Atlas here is displeased with having to stay in the attic, so I sent a little text to Eloise to let the new witch know we'd like our home back when the witch settles in."

The town's coven leading witch is the one who got the notification to expect a newcomer in town soon, one with the deed to our castle in tow and no knowledge of what she is.

Marcus's face falls while Julius, the green bastard, looks seven different shades of relieved over the whole thing. He's the person who makes this castle more home than residence, so I know he must be itching to get back to making his simmer pots or gossiping with Eloise while the pair knit doilies. Marcus grabs hold of Julius' current ball of yarn and tosses it up with a whoop, unspooling the material a few meters.

My eyes linger on the faces of my nest-mates. Something in

their expressions is tense in a way that makes me want to take it all back and just let the damned witch have her way with our home, but I swallow that down. I seem to be the only one in the logical camp of *"Do not let the witch have our home"* when normally we're mostly in sync. Julius is supposed to be the logical, smart one, Darius is supposed to do what's best for us as a whole, and Marcus is supposed to follow the other two with a smile and a shitty joke.

"Now that the secret of supernatural-kind is out, our lives will be vastly different when we leave this attic. Be ready for it," Darius says, his tone flat but his eyes betraying that something of importance is bubbling away in his mind.

CHAPTER I

CHARLOTTE

"Do you know why I've called you into my office, Ms. Ryan?" my boss, Samuel Broadhurst, asks in that condescending tone all pretentious assholes use when they're talking to a subordinate.

Anger prickles down my spine, so I bite my lip, trying to appear thoughtful as I take steadying breaths in through my nose and out through my mouth.

"I believe I'm due for my six-month review, sir," I bite out, an irritated flush rising to my cheeks.

"Correct," he snips out, sniffing a little as he turns in his overstuffed swivel chair.

The man has been in the advertising business for over three decades, and it shows. His office is like stepping into a museum of what once was cool and hip, the bright colors reminiscent of the sixties and seventies with too many textures. The rug under my feet is shag, and the couch in the corner is some kind of crushed velvet —all in colors that make my eyes hurt.

He had an expert eye for what made a good marketing campaign, but suddenly I'm seeing his industry cataracts.

He's not my direct supervisor. He's my supervisor's supervisor, so this is a big deal, or it *would* be a big deal if he hadn't pinched my ass by the water cooler last week and made a comment about all the delectable meat on my bones.

"You see, Charlotte, there are a lot of areas in your portfolio that I find lacking," he says, pulling a large manila folder out from somewhere under his desk.

He slaps it down with a performative *thunk*, and the contents spill onto the desk space between us.

All the ad campaigns I've worked on in my six short months here fill the space between us. Embarrassment heats my cheeks, but I'm proud of these photos. These are hours of hard work and over-time. My supervisor loved these, but clearly Mr. Broadhurst found them lacking.

"I don't see the issue, Mr. Broadhurst."

"Ah, ah. Please, call me Samuel," he croons.

"Um...right, well, what's wrong with my campaigns? These were all approved by Scarlett."

"Yes, but Scarlett's eyes and my eyes are two very different sets, and you see, she may see perfection in these, but I see a stunning lack of vision and fire."

I jerk back in my chair, a little gasp escaping my lips at the severity of his words. These ads are already running, so there is no pulling them back and reworking them. The clients have paid and were happy, but Mr. Broadhurst is the one with the problem.

"I don't understand, the clients all approved of these—"

"And the client is hardly ever really right." He scoffs. "These are fine, amateur at best, but you could really flourish if you were being mentored by me." Mr. Broadhurst gives my body a lecherous look.

It all clicks then. This entire meeting is bullshit.

"Scarlett is my boss and mentor." I skirt around what I really want to say. I need this job so badly it hurts.

"Well, Scarlett," he sneers, "is my underling, and she doesn't yet have the skills I possess." Mr. Broadhurst tosses his arms out and braces his hands on his desk.

The sharp cut of his lime-green suit is too perfect, and it shows all the imperfections of the man underneath. The sweat stains under his arms are clear when his jacket stretches to accommodate his grandiose motions. He's trying too hard to be high fashion for a time that has come and gone.

"Sir, this is not really something I think is necessary. I enjoy working with Scarlett." I try to keep my tone soft and submissive when all I want to do is scream.

He's a creep who hasn't stopped eyeing my breasts in every meeting, who grabs at my ass and tummy when he thinks no one is looking, and who's just out of his dang mind if he thinks I'm interested.

He stands abruptly and rounds his desk before leaning against it so his cock is level with my face. The nearly concave crotch of his pants tells me there is much to be desired in the dick department, but I swallow nervously anyway.

This is not happening. It *can't* be happening. There must have been something in the smoothie I had for breakfast or some kind of hallucinogenic in the hairspray I borrowed from Kennedy.

"Well, since you are so pleased to be working with Scarlett, let's get to the actual point of this meeting, shall we?" he asks with a jerk of his hips in my direction. "If you want to keep this little job of yours, you are going to need to stay later, much later, and attend to...special events on the weekends." He gives a toothy smile that is all too white.

I fight the urge to gag as I shake my head.

"No? So you're fine being fired, then? Have no desire to ever work in this industry again? My industry," he growls and grabs at my shoulder, his spindly fingers digging into my flesh.

"Please let go of me. It's not appropriate for you to touch me," I plead numbly, bile rising up the back of my throat in a slow creep.

"I can touch you however the fuck I want. I own your ass as long as you're employed here. If you want to keep your job and your stupid little cubicle, where you do work that leaves little impact on the world in comparison to mine, you will do what's good for you. Pull my cock out and suck it," he hisses, and I don't know what comes over me.

I vomit.

I vomit all over his hideous suit and his shrimp dick that is way too close to my face.

His responding scream pierces my eardrums, but I can't stop until my stomach is completely empty. Everything vile is purged from my stomach and seemingly my soul. I look up at him, feeling sunken in.

His face is beet red, and the fine hairs that he combs over the balding spot on his head are peeling up. "Get the fuck out! You're fired, you fucking disgusting cow! You will never work in New York again! Get out!"

I lurch out of my seat, nearly knocking it onto the floor as I scramble out of his office, wiping the remnants of my sick from the corners of my mouth.

"Oh my fucking god!" Kennedy squeals, her feet actually kicking out because of her joy at this whole situation.

"My life being completely ruined is a big joke, huh?" I ask, but all the wind has already sputtered out of my sails.

I have to admit. It's just a little funny that I puked all over my former boss's boss.

"Your life isn't ruined, don't be such a fucking brat, Lottie," my best friend and adoptive sister says with a snicker.

She grabs the handle of vodka sitting between us and pours herself another shot.

We're teetering dangerously close to the middle of the bottle, but I'm feeling too good to care that much.

"I was born a brat and will die that way," I say, sticking my tongue out at her.

She laughs so hard that she snorts and winces as a dribble of the alcohol runs out of her nose.

"Fuck! That burns, so bad, in my eyes." She wheezes, fanning her face and trying to get herself to stop laughing.

I bite the inside of my lip so hard I taste blood, but I can't stop myself from laughing. "I'll get you some water."

I shuffle into my small kitchen and pull open the fridge, ignoring the fact that two shelves are missing and that the one that is left only has two-day-old takeout and ketchup of unknown origin. I grab a small bottle of water and bring it back into the living room.

Kennedy is gasping like a fish as her hands flail out. She grabs the water and chugs the little bottle.

"That's what you get for reveling in the loss of my livelihood," I deadpan.

She chucks the empty container at me, and I just let it hit my tit instead of moving out of the way.

"You know they were never going to let you do what you wanted. You can get back into painting now, maybe actually sell some of those amazing pieces you make? How many do you have just sitting in your hall closet?" she asks, arching a perfectly waxed brow.

My adoptive sister is perfect in a lot of ways that I'm not. If she wasn't the best person I knew, maybe I'd be jealous of her golden blond hair, slim figure, and model-like features. She's annoyingly perfect, inside and out, the loveable bitch.

"I don't really think that's what I want to do." I lie through my teeth as easily as I breathe. "I need to get my foot back in the door somewhere. I think all the ad agencies in New York are out unless some brand-new CEO comes on the scene, not knowing the last few decades of things that Broadhurst has influenced," I grumble.

"Or, and hear me out the whole way through"—she jabs her finger at me accusingly—"you move back in with Mom and Dad, they support you while you get your career off the ground, and then we live pretty off the millions you'll make with your art." She says it like she has it all figured out.

When we met in kindergarten, I didn't know the volatile ball of sunshine would become my best friend, but she was persistent. She took me under her wing, drawn in by the shyness that radiated off little me in droves. I had just moved to New York with my parents from Boston, and it was so strange. Everyone was so pretty and bright, and everything was big and loud and smelled weird, but Kennedy took me under her wing and pecked the eyes out of anyone who tried to tell me I was anything other than the best. Needless to say, we remained friends through middle and high school too. When my parents died in my senior year, her family welcomed me with open arms and adopted me when I turned eighteen. So my best friend became my sister, and there has never been a moment of peace for either of us since.

"You're such a brat," I say, flicking her forehead as gently as humanly possible.

She pouts and flips her long blonde hair over her shoulder. "I'm your brat...and ocassionaly the very bratty girl to some very lucky girls, guys, and nonbinary babes." She winks at me, and I snicker. I love how open my sister is...most times.

"And what about you? The big bad world of finance hasn't swallowed you up and turned you into a stooped little goblin yet?"

She rolls her eyes, the brains in her head just as awe-inspiring as her beauty. "As if. I have everyone in that office wrapped around my little finger." She wiggles her pinkie for emphasis.

"I don't think those finance bros are used to pretty women talking to them about things on or above their intelligence level."

"Yeah, probably not, but they aren't all that bad." She shrugs a shoulder. "I think I'm going to hookup with Chad again."

I shiver at the mention of her on-and-off-again fling since college, only now he's Kennedy's coworker—and benefits greatly from being in her orbit.

"Are you sure? Doesn't he actively avoid going down on you?" I ask, pulling from the countless stories she's told me of their less-than-spectacular bedroom life.

"Yes, but that's why I have a vibrator. Unlimited orgasms," she says, though the bubbly excitement in her tone doesn't match her forlorn expression.

"Kennedy, you can't just settle for Chad. If you really want to get a house in the burbs and have two point five kids, a million guys in this city would bend over backward to be yours," I say softly as I plop down beside her and wrap her in a tight hug.

"I'm sick and tired of being lonely, Lottie. I want a love that will take my breath away and orgasms given by another human being." She says with a little sigh, returning my embrace and burying her face in my shoulder.

I hold my sister tight for a long time before my phone ruins the moment, ringing with the same stupid ringtone I've had since high school.

"Who the hell is calling you at nine p.m., on a weekday? Please tell me you've been hooking up with someone but have been too busy to tell me?" She pushes me back, a flush of genuine excitement on her face.

I snicker and shake my head. "As if. You know how the city is—unless you're a size double zero, then you're made to feel like no one out there will love you." I sigh, reaching over and plucking my phone from under the discarded wrappers of all the snacks we've devoured.

I'm not ashamed of my body. I'm pretty, gorgeous even with the right outfit, and I just so happen to be fat. It's not a dirty word, just a damn fact. I'm fat and hot as hell.

13

"Hello?"

The call from a private number is odd, but the whole day has been one gigantic circus.

"Is this Charlotte Ryan speaking?"

The hard-earned buzz from all the vodka and sugar evaporates at the steely, professional tone of the speaker, and I feel like I've been doused in cold water.

"Yes, who is this?" I ask hesitantly.

"My name is Michael Anderson. I'm with Spalder and White Associates. You are mentioned in the will of one of my clients. Are you able to make it into our office tomorrow morning at eight?"

A high-pitched whine fills my ears.

I don't have any family left, so this must be a joke.

"I don't understand," I croak as all the moisture in my mouth dries up.

"You must be feeling a lot of different emotions right now, but there are some incredibly important documents and accounts I'd like to get put into your name as soon as possible. Ms. McKenna was quite clear about how she wanted things to go when the end came."

The notes of warmth and fondness in his voice fill me with an ache of envy that makes me want to puke all over again. There was someone out there who cared enough to leave me some important things in their will but not enough to find me when I had been orphaned?

"Give me that," Kennedy says, snatching my phone, and a few of my hairs. "Who are you and why are you upsetting my sister?"

Kennedy gasps, her mouth forming a perfect *O* as Michael Anderson tells her about me being in someone's will. Someone I didn't know existed and was out there all along, being vaguely aware of me.

She nods once and then again before hanging up.

"So I'm taking you to that appointment tomorrow. He sounds

hot and like he isn't afraid to go down," she purrs, giving me her best bedroom eyes.

CHAPTER 2

CHARLOTTE

"Come on, you look fine," I snap at Kennedy as I drag her toward the gleaming building where the offices of Spalder & White are located.

Apparently, they're bigwigs in the city, and everyone who is anyone uses these hotshot lawyers for any and all legal work. It's like a giant shark tank plopped down right in the heart of Manhattan.

"I need to look more than fine," she hisses, snatching her arm from my hands and fluffing up her soft waves again.

She's dressed to kill in some red-bottomed shoes she bought with her first big paycheck, and a soft-pink pencil skirt that clings to her ample ass and hips but fits tightly to her toned legs. Her blouse is a blush pink, and she's left a few buttons undone at the top to show off her killer rack.

"This is possibly 'catching my future husband' territory. Remember to be nice to all your possible future in-laws," she says teasingly with a wink as she sashays into the building.

I stare at her as two men in thousand-dollar suits practically fight over the honor of opening the door for her before she turns around and gestures for me to follow. The smile on her face is bright, electric, and filled with more charisma than I have in my entire body.

I let my art and designs speak for themselves.

I shove my hands into the pockets of my corduroy pants and shuffle into the building after her. The two men who had been holding the doors open for her nearly let them shut on me, barely even registering my existence.

Kennedy ignores them and links arms with me, giving my shoulder a good-natured pat. "You're going to be fine. I'm with you. Mom and Dad are parked down the street, and we have a reservation at Gino's for when this is all over. What better way to celebrate an unexpected inheritance than with too much pasta and breadsticks?"

I snort, laughter rumbling out of me. "OK, OK, let's go and find out what the person—who couldn't be bothered with me when they were alive—left me."

The brightness in her expression softens, and she gives me a squeeze. "Their loss, our gain."

A stupid grin splits my face, despite my best efforts to force it down. "Yeah, I've got all the family I need."

"Damn right," she whispers before straightening up her posture.

We walk to the elevator and take it all the way up. The whole thing is made of glass and is extraordinarily terrifying, but the view at the top takes my breath away. The sun rising up over New York has never been so beautiful, and I'm seeing it all.

We're greeted by a much younger man than I'd imagined. He's startlingly handsome. His neat black suit and perfectly coiffed dark hair make him look like he should be the one on Kennedy's arm. Possible future in-laws indeed. Even his subtle professional smile accentuates his sharp bone structure.

"You must be Ms. Ryan and Ms. Blackburn. I'm Michael Anderson. It's wonderful to see you both."

"That we are," Kennedy says, pulling me out of the elevator and more into the opulent entry way of the Spalder & White offices.

The two names are written in gold on the granite wall behind a reception desk, where a slight woman sits. Her shiny chestnut hair is a near-perfect match to the glazed oak monstrosity piled high with folders and sticky notes. Her nose is in a book, but Michael doesn't seem to notice, or mind.

"Come right this way. My office is just through here." He gestures to a short hallway lined with impressive doors, each with a shining golden nameplate.

His is at the end, with a window from floor to ceiling behind a massive solid wood desk that I very much hit my knee on as I go to take a seat in front of it.

"Shit," I hiss softly, rubbing at the sore skin.

"I apologize on behalf of my offensive furniture, Ms. Ryan," Michael says as he sits across from Kennedy and me, the smile on his lips softer but professional. "I'm sure you were devastated to hear about the loss of your aunt."

"I didn't know I had one. Your phone call was the first I heard of her." I say plainly.

Mom and Dad never talked about siblings or much of anything. They were immigrants from Ireland and never liked to talk about their lives before they became American citizens. I never pried any further into it when I had the chance, and I was really starting to regret it.

"Oh, I see." Michael nods as he pulls up something on his computer. "Well, I was Ms. Aspen McKenna's right hand when it came to anything legal. She resided in Ireland but had many holdings in the States," he explains before turning the screen toward me.

I sputter at the number of zeros before me.

"You're fucking rich," Kennedy mumbles. "I call being your accountant."

I smack her thigh gently but nod.

"These numbers are why I asked you to bring all your documents. Do you have them?" He extends a hand toward me.

I sling my tote bag off my shoulder and pull out my birth certificate, social security card, and college transcripts. The three documents that apparently make up who I am.

"Fine arts major?" Michael questions as he takes them from me and makes a neat little pile before pressing a button on his phone. "Paisley, I need copies made of Ms. Ryan's documents."

"Right away, sir."

The woman from the reception desk bustles in and quickly takes my papers from Michael's desk before disappearing out the door again.

I should be more worried, but I can't sense the spark of doubt that I normally get when someone is trying to fuck me over.

"Lottie's a very talented artist. Her work is incredible!" Kennedy gushes, leaning forward and pulling her phone from her way too-tiny clutch. "Look, she made me this for my birthday last year." She turns her phone, and I want to melt into the floor.

It's a hyperrealistic painting of a naked Viking man on a horse, riding into battle.

Michael arches a brow, the corners of his lips tipping up. I swear his eyes flick to Kennedy's face as she ogles the picture with a satisfied grin, but it's over so quickly I can't be sure.

In what seems like way too little time, Paisley comes back with two manila folders. She places them on Michael's desk and smiles at Kennedy and me before she leaves again.

"I see the talent," he says and then clears his throat. "Bringing things back to the matter at hand, Ms. McKenna's will contains a conditional bequest—that her beneficiary complete their college education before the assets can be transferred. These documents will speed up the process immensely." Quickly checking both fold-

19

ers, he puts the copies into his desk drawer and hands me back my originals.

"There are more assets than just the cash and investments," he says, flipping through some papers before he pulls out another folder that gives me a brief flashback to my former boss's office. "There are a few plots of farmland and underdeveloped property that will be transferred to you automatically, but the most interesting piece of property in the late Ms. McKenna's portfolio is this." He slides an older piece of paper across the desk.

Kennedy and I lean over in sync to take in the fanciful script on the document. Parts of it are hard to read, but most bits toward the end are incredibly clear.

"I own a castle in Ireland?" I ask breathlessly.

"Indeed, you do, in County Kerry, in the town of Colbéliard."

"Where the heck is that?" Kennedy asks, spine snapping straight. "And does that make her a princess?"

Michael suddenly laughs, the reaction seemingly startling even him. He clears his throat, loosening his tie. "No, that doesn't make your sister a princess. It's an old castle, privately owned and in a livable state. Your aunt had one further condition. In order to complete the transfer of deeds, you'll be required to spend some time there." He pauses and looks at another document sitting on his desk. "This is a direct quote—'Experience the homeland of your ancestors to become your best self.'"

Kennedy smacks her hands over her mouth to keep her giggles in, and I just stare at Michael.

"I have to move to Ireland?"

CHAPTER 3

CHARLOTTE

BETWEEN GETTING on the plane in New York and getting off in Galway, it's like being transported to a different world. Sure, being dehydrated and mussed from oversleeping to get through the flight might add to the sense of a distorted reality, but something in the air buzzes along my skin.

I sigh as I drop into a chair beside the gate, watching as people mill about with direction I just don't have. Colbéliard, my new castle, and the mysterious quest of finding myself await.

As my phone connects to the slow-as-molasses airport Wi-Fi, notification after notification comes through.

"What the—" I grumble as I unlock my phone, trying to take in the biblical-level flood of messages.

I go for the texts over the news and email notifications, knowing my family is going to want proof of life.

Momma Bear: Fly safe, sweetie

> Momma Bear: There's been a big announcement on the news. I don't want you to panic. We're just a call away.

> Pops: You'll be alright. Call me if you have questions.

> Kenny Girl: HAVE YOU SEEN THE NEWS?!?!?

> Kenny Girl: OMG, Of course you haven't. You're probably snoring on a plane and drooling on the shoulder of a stranger.

> Kenny Girl: You know I love you, babe, but when it comes to flying, you turn into an eighty-year-old

> Kenny Girl: Look at your texts first, no news apps until you get through it all!!!!!!!! Mom is freaking out worrying about you.

The panic and confusion that settles onto my shoulders makes me curl deeper into the chair. My breath comes out in sharp little pants, and my heart rate kicks up. I kind of want to puke, but everything around me is too normal to warrant an all-out panic attack before even checking the news.

I leave my messages and click on the first bold banner that crosses my screen.

MONSTERS: FINALLY COMING OUT FROM UNDER THE BED.

A grainy photo, which I assume is supposed to depict Bigfoot, Nosferatu, and a swamp monster, complements the dramatic flair of the headline. I snort, clicking out of the app to check the date. It's not April first, but all this feels like some elaborate prank being played on me by my family. How they got the app on my phone to display that headline is something I'll have to ask about and steal when I plot my revenge, but for now, I call Kennedy.

"Ha, ha, very funny, Kennedy—"

"Bitch, do not even! I take it you didn't see the dragon spewing flames from the torch of the Statue of Liberty? A woman on the news pulled off a very fancy wig to reveal a head full of snakes too! I am losing my shit but am also weirdly fucking excited."

The choking sound that slips from my lips is the only sign I heard her at all. All my normal faculties have stalled. I can't breathe, and my heart races so erratically in my chest I'm worried I'll go into cardiac arrest.

"In through your nose and out through your mouth, Lottie. Please don't pass out in the airport. Well, actually passing out in the airport would be preferable to passing out where you're headed —that rinky-dink little town," she says teasingly, but tension laces her voice.

The city girl is none too pleased about my relocation to the middle of nowhere, Ireland.

I don't know if Colbéliard has an emergency room or even a local doctor. The small town is two hours from Galway, heading south, with nothing advertised except for the castle and the local loch for tourist attractions.

"You still with me, Lottie? Wheeze once for yes and groan for no." My sister-slash-best friend's voice is tight.

She's not a worrier, but this is an unprecedented situation. It's not every day that monsters just...make themselves known.

"You're really not kidding?" My voice is small, fragile in a way that makes me feel exposed.

"I'm not creative-writing class enough to come up with something like this, Lottie." She sighs.

"Is it weird that I'm pleased to be an ocean away from the Appalachian Mountains?"

My question makes my sister laugh so hard she snorts, groaning at the horribly unladylike sound coming from her nose like it betrayed her on purpose.

"Of course, that's the first thing you think about. You may be away from those woods, but Ireland is teeming with its own monsters. Oh, fuck me, I won't be able to ride the subway ever again. I'm fucking terrified of the idea that rat people are real." I hear her shudder through the phone.

"Just have Chad pay for all your Ubers to and from work. Make the finance bro work for you, Kennedy."

She groans across the line in response.

"Did something happen that I don't know about?" I ask, trying to keep up with the subject whiplash common in Kennedy conversations.

"Yeah, apparently he wants us to get serious, like meet the parents and come to holidays and shit."

"But he's the one who insisted you keep it casual?" I ask in faux horror.

Any of those finance bros and literal Chads with half a brain cell would be lucky to snatch up Kennedy if she gave them the time of day. The whole appeal of the actual Chad was that he was cool with flings.

"I know, right?! He said he has reservations with them next week, and he would just 'love for me to meet them.'" She makes her voice more nasally and drops it an octave, giving her best Chad impression.

I hardly know if it's a good one or not. I tend to zone out when he tries to make small talk.

"Tell him no. Tell him to take a long walk off a short pier on Coney Island."

"Even I'm not that cruel." She scoffs, and I roll my eyes.

"You can be when it comes to the numbers. Think of it this way. He's trying to steal away precious time that could be spent riding monster dick. Now that it's out there, you can't just settle for a two-pump chump who doesn't even have the courtesy to get you off with his tongue afterward," I huff, agitation sending tingles racing down my back.

The subtle prickles of static are sharp and exciting as I let myself tell her what's really on my mind.

"Yuh know, I hadn't actually thought of it that way. Look at you, yuh big horn dog, going right for the monster dick and taking no prisoners. Poor Chad is going to be crushed."

"Good. He sucked, and you deserved so much better from the beginning. What do we say to Chads?"

"Not today in my vah-jay," she intones.

Our little spoof of the fantasy TV show tagline never fails to bring a smile to my face.

"Good. OK, I'm going to go. I'm getting a lot of weird looks in the airport, and I think it's just better to rip the Band-Aid off."

"OK, I'm here if you need me. I'll keep my phone on hand, and Mom would love to hear from you. Yuh know, signs of life and all that," she says before smacking a kiss against the receiver. "Love ya, sister."

"Love you, sis." I hang up before I can analyze the burning starting in my eyes and the lump that suddenly welled up in my throat.

I miss her already. This whole time I've been fighting the urge not to miss them, but like a ton of bricks and a bad cold had a sinister lovechild, it always manages to catch up to you in the end.

Once I'm out of the airport, it's impossible not to notice how much cleaner it is here. Even in the city just outside the airport. The drizzle that hangs in the air makes each lungful thicker, but nonetheless, it's sweet.

Maybe Ireland is where I'll magically discover myself and achieve nirvana and all that jazz. If anything, I can make some good art. I've always loved painting clouds. Rain clouds are a particular favorite of mine. The nuances within the many layers of swirling gray have never been something I've been able to resist. There's something so beautiful, so powerful and wild about the rain.

I take a steadying breath before making a mad dash for the open-air taxi stand. Once under the light covering, I rock on my heels a bit, trying not to keep my eyes on any one person for too long. I don't know a lot about Irish mythology and legend or local lore, so I'm being cautious not to offend anyone or anything as I slip into the back of my cab.

"Where ya headed?" the older gentleman serving as my cabby asks, glancing back at me through the rearview.

"I know it's a long way out, but I'm headed to Colbéliard. Would you be able to take me there, or should I try something else?" I ask, suddenly feeling foolish.

A low, sharp whistle flies out from between his lips, but he nods.

"I can take you. It's two hours at a minimum on the roads, and with weather like this, it's a guarantee that the time will stretch on. It'll cost yuh."

His words are gentle, well meaning, but they stir up a bit of rage within me. I'm a woman who was born and raised in New York City. If I can handle a ninety-nine-cent slice going up to one fifty, then I can damn well manage the cost of a taxi.

"Uh, yeah," I say, trying to sound confident. "I just got here, and I'm already exhausted. If you're willing to do it, I can pay whatever."

"I can tell you've just arrived," he says, nodding toward the airport. "Locals usually know better places to be on a Friday night."

I hiss through my teeth. Of course it's after midnight. It's still Thursday back in NYC. Being in a different time zone than my family feels like the least weird thing to happen in the last twenty-four hours somehow.

"Right, um, OK. Let's do this..."

CHAPTER 4

CHARLOTTE

WHEN THE SIGN for Colbéliard comes into view, I give a playful cheer, pleased that the ride didn't feel as long as I had expected after all the day's travel. Stepping out of the cab, I groan as every ache in my body intensifies from staying in one position so long.

"Are you sure you can't drop me off closer?" I ask, voice bordering on a plea.

"Cab won't fit through the narrow roads, love. You'll be fine on your feet. The country air will do you well after all the recycled stuff you breathed on that plane," he says with a little wave.

Huffing, I shut the door and take a step onto the sidewalk. The driver doesn't linger, pulling away from the curb and heading off in the same direction he came.

As I drag my suitcase from the mouth of the little town all the way to the other end, where the castle looms, I find myself out of breath. I have never considered myself athletic, even if I'm a master of jumping to conclusions. Give me a comfy couch, some five-dollar wine, and a paint set over a marathon any day. I may have city legs, but cobblestones for every street is killing me. On the plus side, I've never felt so free among the open spaces of lawns and gardens.

Growing up in the city, I only ever saw green in the parks of wealthier neighborhoods or in small private gardens in the back-yards of those lucky enough to have them. It's hard to imagine the world is like this, but it's right in front of me and I can't help but gape at it. The land the castle sits on looks wild in the darkness, and the space from the gate to the castle proper is lush and beauti-ful, paved with stones covered in thin layers of green.

I suck in a deep lungful of air, crisper and cleaner compared to anything in NYC, as I withdraw the thick bronze key from my coat. It's the only one Michael gave me, so let's hope it works.

When I slip it into the lock, there's a sudden, sharp whistle of wind. It whips around, yanking at my hair and sending it wildly into my face. I sputter as I turn the key, the lock sliding open with a squeal of effort that sends a chill to my bones. Once I hear the clunk of the mechanism opening, I push the gate open with one hand and pry the dastardly strands from my mouth and eyes.

"Great, perfect first impression," I huff to no one in particular.

Michael told me someone should be here to greet me, but he never told me who, just that they weren't a relative. My aunt had been the last of those on either side, so I was out of luck.

I drag my suitcases down the driveway, the hefty cases bucking up as they roll over the bumpy stones and slip between the cracks. My shoulders ache so badly that I'm pretty sure I must have at least partially dislocated one by the time I make it to the grand double doors. Big wrought iron knockers rest on each door, circular with ornamental twists that still somehow feel outstandingly plain for what I expected of a castle. The pair of them stare at me like a judgy local before I grasp one and knock as hard as I can.

The force of my pounding reverberates through me and makes my shoulders twinge. I hiss and drop the knocker. Grabbing my left shoulder, I do my best to work out the pulsing pain, rolling it forward and backward until the joint feels more like it should.

"Oh, fuck, yes," I sigh, my eyes fluttering shut. The relief brought on is too great not to praise.

"Well, it's nice to meet you too, dear," a soft voice says with a laugh, shocking me out of the moment of peace.

A woman with silver hair and cornflower-blue eyes smiles at me. She's wearing a simple knit sweater and jeans and emits an aura of kindness that puts me at ease. How someone can look so put together at this god-awful hour is a wonder.

I know I look like a hot mess express, to put it nicely. There's no way in the world that after an eight-hour flight and my world being turned upside down I could manage anything else.

I offer her a sorry half smile.

"Sorry, I was— My shoulder—" I ramble.

She chuckles, the sound warm and comforting like a hug, and lifts a hand to stop me.

"You don't need to explain yourself. You're the mistress of the castle now. That means you could go about howling like a dog at the moon if it pleases you," she says sweetly, a hint of humor lacing her voice. "Though I would ask that you didn't. Most in town tend to tuck in early since there is a good bit of farmland and the winery opens early for work."

"Right, no howling," I mumble lamely. "I'm Charlotte Ryan."

"Oh dear, where are my manners? Good to meet you, Charlotte. Come in. My name is Eloise Ansbro; I run a little bookshop in town and agreed to be at the castle when you arrived. Mr. Anderson insisted there be someone here whenever you should arrive."

"Bookshop?" I perk up at the prospect of a new place to find good things to read.

She moves to the side, and I grab my suitcases again.

"Just leave those there for a moment, and they'll be handled. Come sit with me and chat for a while. You must feel awfully overwhelmed."

"It's like you're reading my mind," I say with a nervous laugh.

She *looks* human, but I don't entirely know if she is. From what I've read about Irish folklore on the ride from the airport to here, there are a lot of creatures around these parts that could look human.

"Not one of my specialties." She winks, sweeping me from the entryway up a small flight of stairs and into a sitting room already warmed by a crackling fire. To my surprise, the room is fully furnished in an eclectic mismatch of styles. A well-loved solid wood desk sits across the room, and a large plush rug the color of mulled wine covers most of the floor. Four different chairs are arranged in front of the fireplace. I settle into the leather wing-back chair and set my arms on the rests. I can't fight the giggle that rolls out of my mouth.

I feel like a supervillain. I'm only missing the fluffy white cat.

"So, tell me about yourself, Charlotte." Eloise takes the ultra-cushy Chesterfield chair that almost swallows her entire small stature as she sits.

"Not much to tell."

"That can't be true." She scolds me.

"But it is. I mean, I got fired the same day I found out about my aunt's passing. I didn't know about her, by the way. I don't know anything about my parents' families. I don't even know if she was my mother's sister or my father's sister." The words come rushing out like wine from a cask with the plug pulled. "I never expected to find anyone who would want to claim me besides my best friend and her parents. They took me in when my parents passed."

The corners of Eloise's eyes crinkle thoughtfully. She nods for me to go on, and the words keep coming.

"And now, there's this castle and all my aunt's money, which is more than I've seen in my entire life, and this town and—"

"Take a breath, Charlotte. I'm not going anywhere," Eloise assures me.

"I suppose not. I didn't get the keys to the castle yet," I say, the exhaustion taking all the sting from my words.

"Speaking of..." She pulls a ring of probably a dozen keys from one of the pockets on her sweater, offering them to me. "These are the keys to every door in the castle."

"That's a lot of doors," I sigh, taking the keys from her and going through them one by one.

There are over a dozen, and I get anxious just looking at them.

"This place has some rooms that remain untouched but have been kept up well," she says, grasping her chin as she thinks. "You should have a look around and get your bearings, best to learn your way around in the dark in this town."

"Why in the dark?" A cold sliver of fear snakes its way down my spine, causing me to shiver slightly despite my layers and the fire.

Eloise arches a silver brow at me but smiles.

"The electrician should have the power back on tomorrow, so unless you are comfortable traversing by candlelight, learning how to get around as you are is your best bet," she says in a no-nonsense way that makes me purse my lips, feeling like a naughty child. Her smooth Irish accent softens the blow, but only just.

"Right, thanks."

"Of course, I'm also always a call away. I may not have lived here, but I've been in this town my entire life, and I've made visits to this castle a few times when there were community events. I know my way around well enough." She pushes herself up from the chair. "I should be going. My wife and I are having a meal with her parents sometime tomorrow."

"Oh, awesome, cool," I say with a bit of relief. Some places off the beaten path might not be LGBTQ+ friendly, but this town at least is accepting. "I think I will take a look around, try to get my bearings and then pass out."

"You surely have had quite the shock, coming to a new country and the world changing as it has. Though I will say that our little

31

town has always been a bit more magical than the rest of the world." She winks. "Have a good evening, Charlotte."

"Have a good evening, Eloise," I reply, watching her walk out, leaving me alone in the room that suddenly feels far too big for just me.

I sink back into the chair and groan. My eyes flick around the room to the shelves lined with books, most of which have words on the spines written in languages I can't understand, and then to the grand desk on the opposite side of the room, backed by large arched windows letting in beautiful rays of moonlight.

Not only is this whole country seemingly greener, but it has more than enough rain to keep it that way. It's like I've never seen the world in the right colors before, and as an artist, my heart breaks for New York and all of its gray.

I stand slowly, taking in the room one last time before cursing.

"Shit, I need to get my bags. There's no way I'm letting Eloise heft them up the stairs." The thought of the older woman even attempting to pull those into the house makes me want to faint.

I scramble out of the room and retrace my steps, finding the entryway again. The front doors are closed, and my bags are nowhere in sight.

"Weird," I whisper, eyes flicking around. I tip my head to try to listen for any distant noises, but nothing catches my attention.

I'm alone in the castle, and for all intents and purposes, my bags just walked themselves to the room that will be mine. Wherever that is. An uncanny awareness prickles at the edges of my mind. I might be alone, but it doesn't feel that way.

"Get a hold of yourself, Lottie. Ghosts and ghouls and monsters may exist, but it's highly unlikely any would be living in your castle," I say, trying to reassure myself, though the words sound weak.

I turn back toward the stairs, taking in their grand swoop upward. But a big blob of something yellow whooshes across the landing at the top.

Making me nearly jump out of my skin.

I swear it's there, but when I blink, it's gone. Nothing that big should be that fast, and nothing should be in this house with me. Eloise said so...right?

Wrong. She didn't actually say anything about the status of the maybe monsters in the basement.

"Oh my god, I'm freaking exhausted," I groan, shoving my head into my hands and taking a breath. The exhaustion must be hitting harder than I thought. "New country, new home, new life. I can do this."

CHAPTER 5

CHARLOTTE

THE GROUND FLOOR and basement are all clear of supernaturally spooky things, but the number of spiders living in the corners is enough to make me wish that half the kitchen wasn't sitting in the bowels of this castle. It's inhumane to put the place where food is made beside a nest of possibly venomous spiders. But this place wasn't built in the past century, so I should consider myself lucky that it has running water down there.

I shiver as I make my way around, thankful that the sconces on the walls are all electric, so they should help once that goes on.

"Kitchen, storage, wine cellar, all make up a two-story kitchen. I'm all set to sit out an incursion by the common folk." I snicker as I make my way back up.

A prickle that starts on the back of my neck crawls down my back, and I swat at the spot. If there's a spider down my shirt, I'm going to freak out. Oh god... what if it's the boogeyman? He could be real.

I shouldn't be freaking out this hard since I'm alone, but the awareness of a *possible* something is making my insides twist. I swing my eyes around the hallway at the top of the steps down to the basement section of the kitchen. The mix of warmer air and the coolness from the basement must be what is throwing me off. The castle is seemingly well kept, but even a dozen blazing fireplaces can't make castles a consistently comfortable temperature.

I never expected to own property at all, given the economy is at the moment. Praying for a market crash would be incredibly selfish now, but someone suddenly kicks the bucket, and now I have all of this.

My stomach growls, breaking me out of my stupid castle-centric thoughts. I huff and press a fist into my stomach, trying to ignore the gnawing feeling. I should have eaten the dinner on the plane, but the draw of sweet, dreamless sleep was too strong. When nightmares are a regular occurrence, you'll give anything for a night of peace, even if it means you have to skip overly salty airplane food.

"Maybe there's a pizza place or something." I sigh, but the thought makes me giggle.

Any pizza here would be an affront to a possibly real God.

If monsters are real, then why not God? Why not multiple gods?

"Wow, existential much," I say, allowing myself to slip into that comfortable space you go to when you're alone in your house. Talking out loud comes as naturally as thought. "Get a snack in your tummy and then knock out...or find your suitcases and then knock out."

I still haven't figured out where those went while I was talking to Eloise. Sure, I only checked out the ground floor and basement, but I put at least an hour and a half of effort into the search.

Running my hands along the pristine-looking wallpaper, I take the stairs two at a time to get to where I hope there will be a bedroom. But because nothing is ever easy, a dozen different doors on either side line the first hall I come to on the second level.

"This is going to be impossible."

Not as impossible as I thought.

My tried-and-true method of closing my eyes and going with my gut works way too well for me in this instance. I managed to find a beautiful room with fresh linens and my suitcases on the first try. Ignoring the sense of dread that coils in my stomach at the coincidence, I sit on the edge of the bed, kicking off my shoes. Wiggling my toes in the plush carpet distracts me from my hollow stomach until it yowls in displeasure.

I check through the contents of both bags before I'm satisfied. Sure, there was seemingly no one to bring these up, but a rogue panty thief could have been hiding out beside the loch, just waiting for me to leave these unattended. All panties safe and accounted for, I unpack my clothes and set them in the stunning hand-painted bureau. Of course the motif is wilderness, with little animals and flowers. The paint on the flowers and little forest animals is hardly chipped, and I find them charming.

My aunt must have painstakingly restored and kept up so much of this castle when it was under her care. I wish for a moment that I could have known her. Did she live here all alone? Did she have any pets? Did she have friends in town who I'll have to meet and introduce myself to?

"Fuck me, that'll be great." I chuff. "'Hey, I'm Charlotte Ryan. Yeah, oh, you were friends with my aunt? That's great! She didn't want me even after my parents died! Oh, why am I so bitter? Don't know. Just inherited a castle and will be drip fed a fortune with the expectation of 'finding myself.'" I hiss the words out to the fictitious busybody.

Nah, even if she didn't want me, I can't imagine my aunt would have been friends with someone like that. Besides, if Eloise is any indication, then people should be nice around here. Small town, everyone knows everyone, and I'm going to be the odd duck for a little while. Hopefully, just a little while and not for the rest of my life. That would suck ass.

Groaning, I scrub my hands roughly over my face. My whole body aches with phantom and not-so-phantom pains.

I miss my sister and I miss my parents and I miss being able to order delicious delivery pizza whenever I want.

I pull a small bag of flaxseed crackers I grabbed from the airline out of my bag and munch on them as I take in everything in the room. A wealth of details that cost a fortune are all around me—the lace curtains and fine rugs speak of riches and history I can't comprehend. I feel like an impostor, even if this is all supposed to be mine.

It makes my chest a little less tight to think about calling Kennedy tomorrow and telling her about my trip here.

After finishing the last of my stashed snacks, I venture into the chilly hallway in search of a bathroom, poking at some doors closest to this room. Each door is highlighted by wide beams of moonlight that filter through the intricate metal patterns over the windows, like side quests await me beyond the threshold. Bedroom after bedroom after bedroom, until I encounter the first locked door. A noise of confusion and displeasure rises in my throat, but I choke it down. I have keys to every door, but, of course, I left them in my new room.

"I swear if you aren't a bathroom with a soaking tub, I'm going to be so upset when I finally get you open," I growl at the door before turning and stalking down the hall.

I check five more doors, three more being locked, before I find the bathroom I've been searching for.

Modern fixtures greet me, illuminated by the moonlight through yet another decorative window. Bright white and gleaming gold marble on the floor and trendy white subway tiles on the walls all feel like decoration whiplash compared to the antique furnishings and carpets filling the castle. There is both a clawfoot tub that looks big enough to house two or three giants at the same time and a rain shower with...one, two, three, four showerheads.

I float over and turn on the water, glad it comes out nearly steaming. I shuck off my clothes, glad to rid myself of the past ten-ish hours, and step under the blissfully hot spray.

"That's the stuff," I moan, eyes falling shut.

I run my hands over all my curves, rubbing my hands over my breasts and waist, but especially into the place on my hips where the seams of my panties were digging in painfully. I need to skip the thongs when it comes to traveling next time. You live and learn.

The water pressure and heat are just too good. I stand under the various sprays, whimpering as my muscles are massaged. It's almost erotic how damn good it feels after hours of nothing but recycled air on the plane and then a slightly damp drive here.

"I'm going to live right here. Loch witch of the castle, lady of the clawfoot tub, shall be my name," I mumble with a snort of laughter.

I really don't need to come off like that to the rest of the townspeople, but I can't seem to care at the moment. I stand under the spray and then sit when I find a cute little shelf on one side of the wall and soak up all the heat until my fingers and toes resemble raisins.

Slipping out of the shower some time later, I have to grasp the handle for the sliding door before I fall and crack my skull open.

"No bath mats, no towels. Cool, cool, cool, OK," I murmur, bringing my thumb to my mouth and chomping at the nail.

Something about the soft clicking sound of my teeth taking away bits of the nail soothes me, but I stop myself before I draw blood.

"OK, just...carefully." I spread my arms out, trying to use them to balance myself as I step slowly across the marble floor, heading for the door.

I didn't bring any towels, but I can dry off with a loose and comfy PJ shirt or something to keep the good-ish clothes dry for going out shopping tomorrow. I'm going to need a lot of things. The kitchen is basically empty now that I think about it. I would like some actual soap to wash with, even if that sinfully delightful water does a good enough job. I have travel toiletries, so I'm not completely screwed, but the thought of something full sized and fresh wins my mind over.

I reach the door without busting my ass and pull it open. Toddling into the hallway, I shiver, nipples going hard at the change in temperature.

"Fuck, I need to turn on the heat tomorrow."

Back in the bedroom I've laid claim to, I grab my oldest and comfiest T-shirt from my PJ collection and go about toweling off. So far, so good. This first night isn't a total disaster, and I got in one heck of a shower.

Sighing, I wrap my hair in the same T-shirt and pull on another oversized shirt to sleep in, forgoing the underwear. I prefer to sleep with as little on as possible, but if I start seeing yellow blobs—or any color blobs—again, I can't exactly haul ass out of here buck naked.

I snicker, imagining what people would say if I did have to run out of the castle in the middle of the night. Sure, most people would be asleep, but there are bound to be some teenagers in this town staying up past their bedtime, doing broody teen things. And there I go, running out of the castle with all my rolls glistening in the moonlight.

I bite my lip on another snort, rubbing at the bridge of my nose and adding Breathe Right strips to my mental shopping list.

I'll probably discover I need something else, or a good deal of something elses, in the morning, but that's morning Charlotte's problem.

I draw back the heavy blanket and soft-as-silk sheets and slip into the bed, melting into the softest mattress I've ever lain on. My mind was racing before, but at first contact with this bed, all my thoughts are rendered null and void—flown south for the winter.

"Just need a little nap." I yawn, pulling the blankets up to cover me completely.

I fall into a blissfully dreamless sleep as soon as my eyes close.

CHAPTER 6

MARCUS

WHERE'S MY FOOTBALL?

Oh. Oh, no.

My breath stalls in my chest as I try not to draw the attention of my three gargoyle nest-mates. Darius, Julius, and Atlas are all displeased for their own reasons about being stuck up in the older section of the attic. I'm displeased because I forgot my football in my room and have bugger all to do without it.

When Eloise came by in a tizzy, waving her sparking hands around and lamenting about another witch coming to town with the missing deed, I was thrilled. Darius was, of course, skeptical. Atlas, in his constant state of brooding, glowered harder at the prospect of a stranger. Julius just grumbled something about the overabundance of rain being strange, even for this time of year. Unlike the rest of those old boulders my magic is bonded to, I was *and* still am thrilled.

It's not every day you meet a new witch, though meet is not exactly the word I'd use...more like *hide-from-her-in-your-musty-*

attic. I cackle, the thought of trying to say the sentence as one word is just too hilarious.

"Would you quit it? There is *nothing* funny about this," Atlas hisses, tossing back some of his shoulder-length hair.

It falls right back into place, and I snicker again.

"For once, I agree with Atlas," Darius says, crossing his arms over his chest. His deep blue suit is all wrinkled from the hurry of tossing it on when Eloise first arrived.

When a witch comes knocking, you answer. Or else.

"Never thought I'd see the day," Julius says under his breath.

Atlas smacks the back of his head, and they exchange withering glares.

"I don't think this is funny necessarily, just thinking about how I forgot to lock my bedroom door." The lie rolls off my tongue easily, though my eyes start twitching. With them so distracted, they don't even notice.

"Go shut and lock the door as quickly as possible." Darius finally looks over as my eye stops twitching.

Magic warms the center of my chest. The aid of our nest leader will make me even faster than I could have been on my own.

"Sweet!" I cheer, jumping up and pumping my fist in the air.

I trot over to the wooden hatch in the floor and carefully lift it, then begin the slow descent down the rickety wooden ladder. It groans under the weight of my stone body. Even magic isn't able to mask my presence entirely, especially when interacting with inanimate objects.

Man, that would be so cool if it could do that, though. I'd be an absolute beast. Well, I'm already kind of a beast, but on the footie field, I'd be able to pass through the competition with my magic, get right to their goal before they knew what hit them...or didn't hit them.

I snicker again and let the magic settle into every inch of my body. I feel the planes of my face sharpen and the horns on my head grow at least another inch. The yellow hue of my skin glows for a second before I take off like a silenced shot. The familiar corridors of the castle pass by in a fraction of a second as I fly through the halls and make my way down some stairs. When I reach our floor, I pause for a breath, ignoring the glimpse of her out of the corner of my eye.

There she is.

I don't know what whispers that to me, my heart, my soul, or the universe itself, but I hear it loud and clear. That witch is my mate. I can feel it in every ounce of myself. I want to turn and run into her arms, but instead I keep the course.

I dart into my room, shutting the door as lightly as I can. My breaths turn shallow as I close my eyes and summon the image of her. She's so pretty, soft and full. She's not even made of stone, but she's precious, beyond any materials that could be mined from the earth or born of our kind. Her magic permeates the air and tingles on my tongue like popping sweets.

"When I tell Darius, he's going to lose his mind," I choke out, thinking about my nest-mates and our mate.

That's what she is, not just mine, *ours*.

Atlas' reaction flashes across my mind like a strike, and I flinch from the intensity of it. I can already see the curl of his cruel sneer. She's human...well, sorta, and that's not good enough for him. My hands clench into fists at the thought, and I might just have to punch him to make myself feel better. How dare he judge her before even meeting her?

Indignation flares to life in my chest on behalf of our mate, and I take off again, locking the door behind me and getting to the attic in what amounts to a heartbeat. I zip up the ladder, pulling it back up after me.

"Is it done?"

"Well, yeah, course," I say, freezing for a moment, trying to remember what I was meant to do.

Oh, right. My football!

"Bollocks," I hiss.

Darius growls in response. "Did you not lock the door like I instructed?" he questions, his voice that controlled sort of angry.

My balls practically shrivel up in my athletic shorts. I cup them over the material and frown. *I'm going to need these to give our mate a lovely pearl necklace.*

"No, I did that. I forgot my football."

"You have to be fucking kidding me." Atlas scoffs.

"I am very much not kidding you! She could take forever to settle in, and who knows, Eloise could have been pulling our legs about her."

"I doubt that," Julius says, quick to defend the owner of the only shop in town with wool and yarn he deems worthy enough to use. "Eloise is a good woman. She'll let the witch know about us and that this is our home. We'll give her something from the treasury when she returns the deed to us, and then she'll be gone."

"Like she was never here." Darius gives a curt nod.

"Like she was never here?" I blanch.

Crush me now. Turn the fine particles of my stone to dust. I can't live with that now that I know she exists.

Fuck. My entire life until now feels like one giant bruise I didn't know I had until this very moment. Being aware of it finally makes it ache and itch.

"What's crawled up your ass, balls for brains?" Atlas asks with a shitty grin.

My mouth puckers up, and I debate hitting him like I wanted to downstairs. I love my nest-mate, but he's such a pain in my ass.

"What? I didn't say anything."

"No, but your face got all weird." His features scrunch up, as if he's in agony.

"Why are you both making that face?" Julius asks, his hands busy in front of him with some knitting project.

I can hardly track the movements of his forest-green fingers as they race through row after row of stitches.

"I'm mocking him," Atlas says, then yelps when Darius smacks him in the back of the head.

"I'm not making a face. You're being weird." I drop my face into my hands and do my best to school my expression into something else.

Think of puppies and rainbows and the smell of the earth after it rains. The tension in my shoulders melts away like butter under a hot knife, and I can feel the muscles in my face relax. All my hard work almost gets ruined when Darius swings his dour face my way again.

"Separate now." He jerks his head to the side, using one of his exceptionally tall horns to point to the opposite side of the attic.

Atlas rolls his eyes but complies with the command, flipping our leader the bird the entire way.

Pressing my back into the wall, I sink to the floor and rest my chin on my knees. Forgetting my football leaves me with nothing to do but sit with my thoughts.

"I can't wait for the day those two go to blows," Julius says, lowering himself down beside me and sparing me from gazing back into the well of thoughts filled with the pretty witch.

"Darius will win," I say blandly.

"And that's what we need. Atlas has got to accept his position as the youngest and get over himself." He grouses, knitting needles clicking more harshly as he bites out his words.

"Atlas would die if he had to be less broody and melodramatic." I snicker.

I love my nest-mates, but I have to remind myself extra hard when it comes to Atlas.

"You've taken up a broody position too." Julius lifts a brow.

Behind the golden octagonal frames of his glasses, his eyes are intense... like he's trying to read my mind. I grunt, shaking my head. It would be a great thing if he could actually read my thoughts. Then he'd see our mate and understand just why I'm

45

"brooding." She's perfect, and I'm just collecting dust, like an old Christmas tree in the attic.

"I get to sulk a little. I don't have anything to do." I flap my hands in the direction of his knitting and then to Darius and Atlas, who are likewise occupied with their own distractions. Darius doesn't take time for actual hobbies, so he brought an old clock he's been repairing, and Atlas always seems content to sit beside a window and contemplate existence. Being a gargoyle is one of the most frustrating magical middle spaces to occupy. There are those who are made and those who are born, indistinguishable from one another once they reach adulthood and find their nest-mates, but before that, some purists can be wicked bastards.

"Hold my wool?" He lifts his pinkie to point at the little spooled ball between us on the floor.

I scoop it up and blow some dust bunnies off it. The soft material in my hard fingers is a contrast I always love.

"You honor me." I tease him.

Julius snorts and knocks his bejeweled horns against my much plainer ones. The little zip of sensation is more akin to a tickle than pain, but I jump, tail flicking hard against the wall.

"Hold the wool and look pretty, Marcus. Talking isn't necessary," he says with a roll of his eyes as he sets about making...well, whatever he's making.

It's blobby at the current moment, far too shapeless to tell what it will become in a few days or weeks. The jumper he made me last Christmas is still one of my favorites, though I don't get much wear out of it. Can't exactly play footie in a one-hundred-percent wool fiber jumper and expect it to be as nice as when you first got it.

"A blanket?" I ask, hazarding a guess.

"I'm not sure, actually. I was originally going to make a wrap or a scarf, but then I got distracted and added too many rows, so now it's just...actually, yes, it's going to be a blanket." He smiles. "Have any use for it?"

Building a beautiful nest for our mate.

I shrug a shoulder, trying to keep the heat bubbling in my magical blood from flushing my cheeks a bright orange. I cough to cover the swell of feeling and nod.

"I'll figure some use out for it. I'd like it a lot."

"Consider it yours, then."

I'm going to lose my mind.

Rhythmically, I whack my head against the wall, careful to keep from bumping my horns too hard, while keeping the enormous ball of wool Julius is still working with off the floor. As fun as it is to imagine making a nest to present to our mate, I would rather be actually doing it! We have more than enough rooms. We could even knock down some walls and make an even bigger room! Or we could move some things around and put her in one of the larger former common spaces. I wonder if she would like the dungeon since it's underground and you can feel the magic in the walls.

"You're thinking really hard over there," Julius says, not lifting his eyes from his stitches.

His wings are tucked neatly behind him between his back and the wall, tail draped loosely over his legs with the tip swishing back and forth slowly. He always looks effortless and at ease, but he's sharp and catches everything.

"The witch," I admit, swallowing the drool that fills my mouth at the thoughts of her beautiful body.

What does her voice sound like? Does she know any sex spells?

"What about her?"

"Do you think she's nice?"

"Doesn't really matter if Darius gets his way. She'll be gone before we know if she's nice or not."

"But what if we don't just pay her for the deed? Or maybe she won't want to give it up!" I whisper-yell. "What if she has us do trials to get the deed back, to prove our worth?"

"This isn't the old days, Marcus. I doubt she'll actually be that fun."

I scowl. "I bet she's a lot of fun."

"On what basis do you hedge that bet?" he asks in that incredibly smart-ass way of his.

"Can't I just have a good feeling?"

"You can, but we both know you have an instinct for hunting and sport. You're not the people person of the nest." He smoothes out a nonexistent wrinkle on the collar of his finely pressed dress shirt.

"You're not the only people person. People like me." I argue with him.

Julius chuckles, settling the half-made blanket in his lap along with the needles. "You're being fight-y. Care to share exactly why?"

Damn perceptiveness.

I could lie, but again, a bad liar versus a very perceptive nest-mate does not make for a good outcome.

"I saw her," I murmur.

"The witch?" Julius asks, his eyes sparkling with interest.

"Yes, the witch."

"Which witch?" Darius questions, the magic within our bond crackling from his anger.

CHAPTER 7

CHARLOTTE

I'м a big fan of sleep. It doesn't really require anything, but shutting off my brain is something I can always do. I sigh, rolling over in the bed and tangling myself further into the incredibly decadent sheets and blankets. I never would have splurged on something this undoubtedly expensive for myself, but since it's already here, I allow myself to enjoy it.

"I could probably afford to have this entire bed shipped to Kennedy so she could feel how unreal it is." The thought flows past my lips with a snicker.

I could, but I won't. Something deep inside me bites down on the idea, sharp gnashing teeth refusing to part with a single part of this castle.

My castle.

I jolt up, one of my tits popping out of the stretched-out neck of my oversized shirt and nearly slapping me in the face as I rip myself away from the thought.

"Damn it." I yank my shirt off over my head.

The day needs to get started anyway, and why not just dive into it with some clean clothes...well, clean-*ish*. As an artist who doesn't have time to change or find a smock, all the items of clothing I own get paint stains.

I fumble from the bed, feet not wanting to escape their tangle in the sheets, until I'm nearly face down on the carpet. I force myself to stand and groan, my back popping sharply.

"Fuck, that felt so good," I moan, rubbing at my eyes, trying to wake myself up quickly by any means possible.

I grab my phone from the charger, shoot a quick "here and safe" to Mom and Dad, then send Kennedy a text with a picture of the view beyond my window. The loch and lush green banks, drops of rain rolling down the window. I manage to keep my naked body while giving her a peace sign in the old warped glass.

With the task of providing proof of life taken care of, I set about dressing. I groan as I clasp my bra and pull on a band tee with a few dried paint splatters from the first drawer. I barely fight the urge to toss on a pair of overalls and just decide *fuck it*. It's the simplest way to feel and look mostly put together, and after all the fun of yesterday, I need something simple. I have several pairs of overalls, and each one has their own quirks. This is a favorite of mine, with patches made by some artist friends as a part of art trades.

I absentmindedly pick at some of the loose threads of a death's-head moth on my thigh before I tug on my shoes. Shuffling around in my carry-on bag, I snag the shiny new black card Michael gave me before my trip. He said the balance was "yes," and I'm more than ready to see what that means.

Sweat and drops of atmosphere cling to my brow as I push into the only shop in town that has a nonpractical purpose. Books, Bits, and Baubles is incredibly charming. The shop, painted bright blue with quaint brown shingles, is situated on what I've gathered is the main street of Colbéliard. There are two grocery stores, a butcher shop, some various farming goods stores, and a trinket shop that is as gray as the oncoming clouds, but Books, Bits, and Baubles is bright and fun.

The bell over the door announces my arrival with a sweet little chime. The smell of melting wax, amber, and apples stops me in my tracks. Something about the scent sits in my chest, warming me to my bones.

Eloise stands behind the counter, an apple in one hand and a knife in the other, which she waves in my direction.

"Come in now, Charlotte. No reason to be letting in the breeze." She chides gently.

I step in, and the door snaps shut behind me, the open sign banging against the window sharply.

I grit my teeth and wince. "Sorry."

"Not a problem. That door has been through far worse. How is your first day in town?" she asks with a grin, placing the apple on a little wooden plate and slicing it with the knife.

"Um, well, I got some groceries delivered to the castle so I can stock up on some things," I say, feeling more than a little weird ordering so much considering I don't know how long I'll be staying.

I don't want to go into town if I don't have to, so buying the biggest bulk packs of rice, noodles, some beans, and flour was a good start. I could basically live on that, some fats and potatoes, until Michael has deemed I've fulfilled the terms of the inheritance. Then I can go back to New York. I want to buy a place to live where Kennedy and I can room together again, and then maybe a studio. A big "fuck off" space where I can throw paint at the walls if I want.

"Smart, the weather has been fairly"—she purses her lips, turning a discerning eye to the deep gray clouds in the sky—"shit

51

for the most part since you've arrived, but really, all this greenery needs to be watered, and the Gods do that for us."

"Gods?" I ask with a little squeak.

Sure, monsters are real. Vampires, werewolves, mummies, fairies, oh my; so I guess multiple gods really are in the cards. Still, to have this mostly normal-appearing older woman going all polytheist on me out of nowhere shocks the hell out of me.

Eloise smiles, the corners of her eyes crinkling slightly, before she gestures to a chain hanging around her neck with the tip of her knife. A drop of apple juice rolls down the sharp edge of the blade. My eyes follow it to a set of three swirls in a triangle formation, each section made of a different precious metal.

"Pretty necklace," I say, rubbing the back of my neck.

"It's a triskele, not claimed solely by the Celtic pagans, but used a damn lot in our symbology."

"Pagan, that's cool, so you and your wife practice?"

"We do indeed, all the holidays and rituals too." She chuckles softly at my wide-eyed expression. "She works at the butcher's shop down the street. Brought the concept of the charcuterie boards to town." The pride in her voice makes me blush.

The other woman isn't even here, but I almost feel like I'm intruding. It reminds me of how the lust-struck guys that Kennedy had around spoke about her. Like she hung the moon and crafted each of the stars.

I bite my cheek to keep from asking any other dumb questions or making a stupid comment about how *cool* she is. That type of love feeds my desire to feel the same one day.

I let my eyes wander, taking in the cute, kitschy little shop. Books, Bits, and Baubles is an apt name for the space dominated by bookshelves labeled by genre, baskets filled with spools of yarn in every color, and tables filled with trinkets that lack purpose but look cute.

"Have a browse around. Don't let an old woman chat your ear off." Eloise waves me farther into the shop.

"Thanks, this place looks like a lot of fun," I say before cringing internally.

I'm not the best with my words. I'd much rather throw some colors on a canvas.

That's what I need. Art supplies.

A dozen neatly wrapped parcels are waiting just inside the door when I get back to the castle. The shopkeepers did say they delivered, but I never expected the stuff to arrive back at the castle before I did. I really didn't expect it to arrive inside either. *Not going to think about that.* The food stuff is separated from the art supplies in neat piles I would be way too lazy to bother with. *This is too weird.*

I grab the paints and canvas I got at Books, Bits, and Baubles. Then I head in search of the room with the best light.

If I had to guess, this was the armory. Ancient-looking pieces of armor still hang on the walls. From breastplates to helmets, shields, and bracers, beams of light constantly reflect off the polished pieces right into my eyes as I try to find a suitable spot for my new painting area. Toward the back of the grand space is a small alcove with windows on all sides of the semicircle-shaped nook. Heavy velvet curtains frame the windows, their gold accents glittering as they catch the light.

"If I put that weirdly cut drop cloth down right here..." I run my fingers through the air as I imagine the space filled to the brim with my supplies, the sunlight as it is right now, and the peace to do the work I love. "It's perfect," I sigh.

Setting up the easel, canvases, and then all my paint sets takes enough time that the sun has started to set. The view makes me itch to pick up a pallet and mix colors to match, but I put the urge aside as my stomach audibly growls.

"Guess I'll actually have to make use of all that food I bought," I huff.

Cooking is an art form I've never mastered—nor wanted to take the time to try.

I lumber out of my beautiful new studio, dragging my feet as I shut the thick curtains and plunge the space into darkness.

The air fizzles in my lungs, and I have that feeling at the edge of my consciousness again. *I'm not alone in this house.* Whatever is here hasn't made its presence known yet This was certainly the devil I didn't know.

"Fuck, please don't be the actual devil," I whimper as I sprint from the room, nearly knocking a set of bracers to the ground in my rush.

The armor turns into mirrors, projecting back my terror blended with shadows. My twisted visage makes theater mask–level expressions of fright.

My feet pound on the stairs as I return to the entryway to get the packages that had seemed less important compared to the art supplies.

A startled laugh explodes out of my mouth as I take in the empty space.

"Great, the devil is stealing my food!" I snap, throwing my hands in the air as if to ward away the food-stealing jerks.

My heart is racing in my chest, but you don't show fear to wild animals, so showing it to evil spirits should have the same rules.

I pull out my phone and scroll through the numbers I collected during the day, mostly shop owners and Eloise's friends, until I find one for a takeout place in town. I shut my eyes to help me recall earlier in the day. The signs on the doors of the restaurants in town advertised short open hours and weird days off but were good to keep in mind if I was feeling lazy. The only place I remember seeing open on Saturday night was a pizza place.

My thumb, guided by hunger, presses call.

"McGnash's Tasty Pies, how can I help you?" The thick

brogue on the other end of the line gives me a momentary pause before my stomach howls its displeasure. "You that new cailín in town?"

"I think so. I don't know what that means."

"Then you are she—" The man on the line laughs heartily. "I'm Seán Walsh, co-owner of this fine establishment."

"I met the McGnash half earlier," I grumble, that same traitorous thumb flitting to my lips. I gnaw on my nail. "Can I have a pizza?"

"Course you can. What toppings do you want on it?"

"I don't take it you have Canadian bacon?" My voice is thin and embarrassed around the question.

"Ah, no, we don't really, but I think I could get some ham from Dara, and it'll be about the same thing. How does that sound?"

"Perfect, thanks. Make that a large pizza, please."

I'm going to need the extras until it's socially acceptable to go out for another order of groceries now that mine have been pilfered.

"It'll be ready for delivery in an hour. This order is on us, welcome to town."

As the line disconnects, my shoulders sag, and every ounce of nervousness from being out and about today crashes into me all at once.

When I was prepping my supplies, nothing else mattered but the color, consistency, and range I was developing as the ideas bubbled away in my head. I wanted to paint big landscapes and show off the colors all around me, but at the same time, I was too caught up with all the little things—the flowers and stonework and people— to dive right into something so big.

I decided that my first project in this new space would have to wait until I had food in my stomach. No good ideas came from a place of hunger. At least, not mine. If I went into ideation like this, then all I would be able to paint would be pastries and cake, like the ones in the window of the grocery store.

My mouth waters as I remember the glittering icings and sugar decorations that sat delicately along the carefully appointed layers of cake.

"Fuck, too hungry, too hungry," I groan and press a hand to my stomach.

I eye the time on my phone and decide against calling to check on the pizza. The last thing I want to do is seem too pushy.

I debate calling Kennedy, but the time difference is another thing I'm getting used to. I'm ahead by a few hours, and calling her in the early evening is just about lunch for her. I know my sister better than most people in the world, and if I were to call her now, she might just be at lunch with Chad.

I don't know why I'm surprised to hear the soft chime of a doorbell, but I am. After a single night and some scattered hours of days, I've almost come to expect some great thunderous booming from the door knockers when my pizza arrives.

Pulling myself from my sketchbook and the cozy spot I've made by the window in my selected bedroom, I tiptoe down the hall. I'm not used to living alone, so my volume goes down with the sun. I'll have to teach myself that it isn't necessary.

CHAPTER 8

JULIUS

I DON'T REMEMBER DOZING off, but when I come to on the old sofa, my knitting has been discarded on a dusty storage box lid, and in its place, Marcus is dozing partially in my lap and partway on the sofa. We're intertwined together, his tail across me and wrapped around my left wrist while he leans heavily against my right. The steady puffs of his breath against the crook of my neck give me goose bumps. Sighing, I extract my hand to stroke his hair softly as he naps against me.

We've always been close for nest-mates, and without physical intimacy, we both would have lost our sanity ages ago. Our relationship is more than just the physical needs being met but not so much as a lover—having someone so steadily by your side in and out of danger forges a bond deeper than words.

Marcus is my favorite unknown integer.

Darius is giving him the cold shoulder for some assumed mistake he made while getting his football, and Atlas has been pretending neither of us exists. The youngest gargoyle among us does so when he gets in a mood, so it's been some days.

"Pretty, pretty witch—" Marcus sighs, nuzzling farther into my neck. His mouth is hot against my chilly skin, and I swear I feel a flick of his tongue before he jolts awake. "Oh...Julius, fuck, sorry."

"It's OK." I chuckle, gently twisting my fingers in his hair. I drop my voice, leaning our foreheads together. "Tell me about the witch."

His eyes go bright, and his tail curls tighter around my wrist. "I only saw her for a second, but I felt her, could taste her magic, and it just tasted...felt like she belongs with us."

His tone gives me pause, hopeful and bright even as a whisper. I'm hesitant to bring up the *M* word, but it's on the tip of my tongue to ask him. My eyes flick to Atlas, who is glaring out the window, before returning to Marcus.

It's exhilarating and terrifying. A witch as our mate would mean that our nest as a whole will be tested. Atlas has his own trauma dealing with witches, Darius is someone who needs control over magic, and Marcus...as great as he is, he can be reckless. A witch's magic is different from that of a gargoyle's on so many levels—it's like comparing an apple to an egg. If she were our mate, then our magic would be entwined. Where she ended and we began would be too blurry to compute.

I'm already getting ahead of myself.

"Can I taste her off you?" I ask, pressing a thumb lightly into his bottom lip as I cradle his jaw.

"Thought you'd never ask, Julius." He slams his mouth to mine, nearly knocking my glasses off as he attacks me with his kiss.

He gives me no time to breathe before shoving his tongue past my lips to stroke at mine. A moan rattles out of me as I grip him closer, his body quickly twisting and moving so he can straddle my lap. A soft, sweet, and earthy taste followed by a fizzle, a crackling on his tongue, draws me in deeper. Her magic is delicious from his lips, and I kiss him in steady sips to savor it.

He groans, fisting my sweater like he can't get close enough. With our nest-mates here, we really can't get any closer, so I draw away from the kiss slowly. My lips tingle from the intensity and from *her*.

"Great, now I've got a boner," Marcus grumbles.

CHAPTER 9

CHARLOTTE

For a small town in the middle of nowhere, Ireland, they make good pizza, so I order again for dinner tonight. I should probably be looking for my groceries, but I'm too spooked to go back down into the kitchen again. *Who has a kitchen that's two floors, anyway?* Me, now, I guess.

The doorbell startled me from my thoughts.

"Coming!" I bellow, doing my best to project my voice through the expanse of halls that lie between me and the front entryway.

I scramble from the rumpled pile of blankets I nestled into to work in my sketchbook. My toe catches on the edge of a rug, and I try not to trip over my feet. An indignant little squeak rips itself from my chest, but I use the momentum of the near fall to clamber down the hall and find myself in the entryway faster than I expected. I don't know if it's my fluffy socks or the carpet, but I nearly eat the wood of the front doors when I don't slow down. My hands slap hard against the unyielding surface, and I fumble for the knob. Pulling open the door, I thrust out a fistful of crumpled euros, my eyes shut against the glare of my embarrassment.

"Well, that's a nice tip, dear, but it's not necessary."

"Eloise?" I yelp. "I thought you were my pizza."

She chuckles and gives a light roll of her eyes, handing me back the bills. She gestures into the castle. "May I?"

"Uh, yes, come in." I scamper out of the way and peek out behind her.

It's so dark now that the sun has started to set. No streetlights to pollute nature. It's so fucking weird, and who knows what's out there?

"I don't normally make social calls after six in the evening, but there is a bit more about this castle that I haven't told you as of yet." She releases a heavy sigh, patting one of the old wooden banisters.

"Oh god, is the castle a giant monster house?" My eyes shoot up to the light fixture that in *no* way resembles a uvula.

"No, but the attic is full of 'em at the moment." She folds her arms over her chest.

"The attic?" I swear my voice won't stop coming out in a demented squeak. The fear has gripped my windpipe and refuses to let go.

Fear of what, exactly? Unknown roommates more so than their probably very monstrous forms.

"Yes, the attic. Those boys don't know their horns from their tails, I swear." She titters. "But they want to meet you and work something out. They want their rooms back."

"They have rooms? They've been here the whole dang time I've been? They've been touching my stuff, haven't they? Oh my god, am I the one stealing space here? I thought my aunt owned this castle."

My words are coming out rapid-fire, and I hardly have a chance to draw breath before Eloise raises her hands like she's trying to approach a startled animal. I knew I wasn't going crazy. The feeling of something or someone else in the house was too real, and there were too many coincidences.

"There has been a little bit of magic and divine intervention involved, I believe. The woman who left you the castle never actually lived here but used magic to gain the deed. The four men who reside in this house are its sworn protectors and the sworn protectors of humankind. There is nothing to fear from them," she says slowly, her eyes locked onto my face.

I try to keep my expression neutral, but I feel like I'm being told the Power Rangers are real, along with Santa and Satan.

"So...do I have a place to live for the foreseeable future?"

Do I have to live with monsters?

I hold that burning question in with my breath.

"Yes, of course." Eloise nods, her expression tightening for a moment before it softens entirely. "These boys just don't want to have to act like mice in their own home. That is a direct quote from the text I received, and I'm just here to do the introductions."

"Oh great, lovely, I like 'not mice,'" I grumble, running my hand through my hair, trying to keep from pulling the strands from the root.

The pain would be a welcome distraction from all the weird bullshit, but the last thing I need is to give myself a bald spot just because of some monstrous men.

"Fantastic. So, let's go to the sitting room, and I'll send off a message to Darius. He's their alpha, the leader of their group."

The word is out of her mouth, and I snort a laugh in nearly the same instant. Alpha, he's their alpha, and now all I can wonder is if they have an omega and a nest somewhere. Kennedy has been forcing me to read way too much omegaverse.

Eloise bristles slightly, and I swear strands of her hair whip around in a nonexistent wind before she settles and begins walking through the castle toward the sitting room.

Glancing back at the door, I groan and open it slightly, trying to will the pizza to get here more quickly. I'm no good on an empty stomach, and I'm going to need cheese and carbs to get through this.

I take the same large leather wingback chair I selected the first time we sat in this room, nestling myself in as deeply as I can to try and disappear, but Eloise simply shakes her head at me.

"They are all fine men, I assure you. I wouldn't have allowed them to meet you otherwise, but I will warn you they aren't... typical."

"Well, duh, they're monsters," I blurt.

"I'm a monster too, I suppose." She crosses her arms slightly over her chest and gives me a look of disappointment that can only be bestowed by a mothering figure.

Damn it.

"I'm sorry, but you said horns and tails and most things in the real world...well, the safe mortal world doesn't have those things," I ramble.

"Snakes, lizards—" She begins, holding up her fingers with each example.

"OK, yes, those things exist, but like...they tend to be much smaller than me."

I shiver and snatch a thick, knitted blanket from a basket beside the chair. I arrange it over my lap, tucking it into the sides of the chair, like sealing myself in will keep the monsters out. I feel like a child trying to pull any sort of imaginary defense from my arsenal to protect myself.

"I'm going to send Darius a message now. He and the others of his nest will join us in a moment," she says, turning her attention to her cell phone.

"What kind of creature groups in a nest? Are they birds? Werewolves or something?" I ask, trying to keep my voice from bubbling up with my laughter.

I cough, trying to dislodge the urge, but it sticks in the back of my throat.

"You'll see. I promise everything will be fine." She reassures me as her fingers fly over the screen for a solid minute before she sets her phone back down in her lap. "All done." She smiles sweetly, like she's not about to completely upend my world for the third time in less than a week.

JULIUS

I don't know what I was expecting to find when we entered the room where the witch waited with Eloise. But I can't say that finding the newcomer bundled under the blanket I made Darius for Christmas last year was on that particular bingo card. I nearly stumble when I see it draped across her lap.

"Ah, and here they are. Charlotte, these are the gargoyle protectors of the castle and, I suppose, part of the world."

Eloise is always too modest and far too immodest at the same time. Sure, we have a duty to protect humankind, but in recent times, that has scaled way down and left me a ton of time to improve my baking, which I'm thankful for. Though with the revelation that supernatural creatures are living among mortals, I know that things are going to change. However, this witch, is not the change I expected to see.

"You give us far too much credit, Eloise," Darius says, sweeping into the room with the grace only he can muster at a time like this, tail and wings tucked behind him primly with his head held high to display his massive horns.

He places a swift kiss on the older witch's cheek before turning his eyes to Charlotte. The witch sinks deeper into our alpha's chair with a squeak.

It was decided we would go only seventy-five-percent monster to meet this new witch, as she is new to the world of the supernatural and we didn't want to give her a heart attack seeing the one-hundred-percent version of us just yet. This is the form we most naturally take, but it's still so odd to see the colors of our flesh contrast against that of a mortal being. Darius is blue, light and powdery and veined with a striking white. Marcus is yellow, bold and as brash as his personality. Atlas is all black, shot through with veins of graying white and darker black. My skin is green like pine needles, with some lighter striations and flecks of black and softer white. I'm very middling in comparison to the brashness of my nest-mates, and it shows.

"My name is Darius Colbéliard, for lack of a proper surname. I am the leader and alpha of the nest of Colbéliard. These are my nestmates Marcus, Julius, and Atlas," he says as he points to each of us in turn.

"So nest is just a word you use. A nest of gargoyles?" the witch asks from her half-hidden position under the blanket.

She tugs it up to her neck when Darius begins to move closer. His steps carry him almost to her feet, which she has tucked up in his chair. She buries herself in the blanket Julius made until we can only see her eyes.

"Yes, nest is the right word. Yuh know, for the group of us, that is, one gargoyle or a nest of them, like a murder of crows. *Cawww.*" Marcus' words are a rapid-fire mess, punctuated with a terrible imitation of a crow.

I bite back a chuckle at how adorable he can be and give a playful wince.

Darius and Eloise join me in the pained motion.

Atlas trudges in behind our brightly colored marigold nest-mate and punches him in the arm. The flash of Atlas' dark stone against Marcus adds to the intensity of the blow.

The sound of stone hitting stone makes Charlotte jump, and the snarl on Atlas' face probably doesn't exactly put her at ease either.

"He'll be fine, it's the state of his brain I'm worried about," Atlas snarks.

His dark eyes are slightly hooded, and in the low light of the sitting room, it's hard to tell that his eyes even have whites and not just endless darkness.

Seventy-five-percent monster mode means that we get the colors, the wings, the horns, the tails, and killer cheekbones but maintain a slightly human look. Atlas isn't doing his best to maintain that small percentage of human appearance that would make Charlotte more comfortable.

"Atlas, I'm sorry I took your house. I didn't know it was your house, but I've moved all the way from America, and I kind of can't go back until I've found myself—whatever the hell that means. My aunt wanted me to discover myself and my family since I guess she knew my parents never talked about it, which is really weird—"

I barely see the witch take a breath as she talks. Maybe she has some type of double lungs?

"Charlotte, all those finer details are for later. For now, let's just get introductions settled and—"

The doorbell cuts off the older witch in her attempt to settle the younger one, who burrows back under the safety of the blanket.

"My pizza!" Charlotte wails, followed by a beast growling from under the blanket.

"Was that your stomach?" Atlas asks with a sneer.

"I haven't eaten all day, and someone stole all my provisions!" she snaps right back, though in the form of a blanket ghost.

"Stole your provisions?" Darius asks slowly, swinging his eyes to me.

Eloise slowly rises from her chair and edges out of the room, hopefully to get the pizza. I wish I could join her, but instead, I have to deal with this weird situation.

"I enchanted the castle a while ago to put away all the groceries. I get lazy sometimes," I reply with a shrug, pushing the golden rim of my glasses back up the bridge of my nose.

This form has them sliding all over the place without a bit of soft skin to grip. But I keep them on for this interaction even if I don't really *need* them. They're as much a part of me as my wings or my tail.

"So where are my things?" she asks with what I can only assume is a tilt of her head under the blanket.

I curse myself for making it so thick and luxurious. I curse myself for making it at all. From the small glimpses I've caught of her, the witch is beautiful, and if I *have* to have an unexpected roommate, it could be worse. I want to see her again, to drink my fill of her features.

My heart does something it hasn't done in a very long time. Beating like a racehorse after the starting gun, the silly thing flips. My stomach then follows suit and swoops as Charlotte drops the blanket into her lap and finally looks at all of us.

She is exquisite.

Her figure is full and plenty curvy, highlighted by the soft drape of her sweater. Dark brown hair and hazel eyes give her soft face that needed depth. Pink lips more suited for whispering sin than spells complete her incredibly charming girl-next-door air. I want to ruin her and be ruined *by* her, but I don't let my fantasies choke me up.

"In the kitchen, exactly where they should be. Did you get any refrigerated items?" I suddenly feel a great need to please her.

Marcus scampers up beside me and grins, looking between us before settling his eyes on her. I can practically hear the little cartoon hearts popping up around his head. "If anything is missing, we'll get it for you. Promise, Julius was just trying to help."

"Um, I got some milk and cheese and a few meat things from the butcher," she murmurs.

I push my glasses up, my jaw ticking slightly. "My spell isn't exactly a complex one. Gargoyles don't have as much magic as witches in that way, but the spell should have put everything in the refrigerator, at least. We can sort things out for the freezer another time."

"So...I just buy stuff and can leave it around."

Atlas barks a laugh as I wince.

"I would much prefer not to. The spell is a fail-safe. In the earlier days when we could actually do our intended protecting job—"

"We will explain more of that later," Darius adds in quickly.

His expression is stony, but his posture is surprisingly at ease.

"Right, later for the details, but I made it in case we were coming in with something and needed to go right back out. That sort of thing. I like to keep the place clean."

"Obnoxiously clean. Without a speck of dust on anything," Atlas says in a way that I know is meant to be mocking but just makes him look like an arsehole.

"Fuck off," I mutter, folding my arms loosely over my chest.

Charlotte blinks at the lot of us. I can see the gears of her mind whirling, trying to make sense of everything before she leans back and stares at Darius.

"I'm not moving out of the room I've picked. It's mine. I drooled on the pillows."

CHAPTER 10

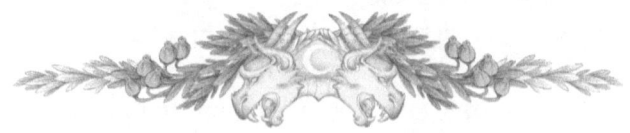

DARIUS

I AM a master of keeping my cool, but when the little witch before me says she wants her room because she's drooled on the pillows...I laugh. I laugh so hard it makes the room shake a little, all the old books and paintings shivering in place, before I catch myself and stop.

"Forgive me." I pause to inwardly check on the magic flowing between myself and my nest-mates and find it glowing. "That has never happened before."

"You've never laughed?" she asks with a smile that can only be described as shit eating.

It reminds me of Atlas, and it just makes our magic glow brighter.

"You'd think, but he laughs at his own jokes far too much," Atlas pipes in, moving from the darkened corner of the room more into the light.

He cuts a striking figure in comparison to the rest of us, all dark in ways our colors are brighter. He's also always been a lot better with night patrols when those weren't a thing of the past. The future is so confusing now that we're known entities in the world of mortals. Perhaps the witch can help us...re-assimilate in some ways.

"I see," Charlotte says carefully. She narrows her eyes on Atlas, her proverbial hackles raised.

I try not to feel slighted, but it does ache a little. As the alpha, there's a lot of posturing one must do to keep the others in line, but this is all out of my control. Atlas is my nest-mate, but Charlotte—this witch—is unknown to us and could be capable of magic that even any manner of magic. As the oldest of the lot, I know there should be an increased sense of caution until we can get more information on her.

"Is that right?" Atlas asks, crossing his arms tightly over his chest and turning his hard stare into a full glare.

The edge of his lips quirk up into a sneer, and that's what snaps the tension like a taut bowstring.

"I see, you're the full-of-yourself one, huh?"

"She's got you pegged!" Marcus howls with laughter, and his wings beat as he leaps across the room and kneels at her side. "You're funny, Charlotte. I like that a lot."

She blushes a deep crimson and flicks her eyes to Marcus, taking him in now that he's closer. He's the best person for her to be close to at the moment. He made himself known to her before, so maybe him showing what a fucking goof he is will keep her calm.

"I've seen you before, haven't I?" She lifts a hand and very gently ghosts it over his jaw.

Marcus closes his eyes, and it's like she's stroked his dick instead of the air in front of his face. "Yeah, I forgot my football and went to get it to keep busy. I've got a lot of energy."

"I bet," she giggles.

"Lots of energy and fuck all to do with it until now," I say, trying to insert myself back into the conversation. "We are going to be working out a new sort of schedule. If we are allowed to be protectors again, then we will not slack in our duty."

"Who gave you such a duty?" Charlotte asks with a smile on her face that is nearly too big, like she's holding back a laugh.

I roll my eyes lightly, trying to lock down the smile dying to climb onto my face. She's beautiful, and it's beginning to get under my skin. She looks so soft and comfortable in my chair. I want her to be well tucked and settled—but next time in my lap.

"Some gargoyles are born, and others are made. From the dawn of time itself, we've only ever had one real purpose: to protect those who need it. No one gave us this duty, it's our whole reason for being," I explain, trying not to feel like some monologuing superhero. "Other monsters have joined us, but we were the first."

"You're born knowing your life's purpose?" she asks, tone becoming a little exasperated. "Lucky ducks."

"I wouldn't say that exactly." Julius rubs the back of his neck and smiles lazily. "We were born to do it, we're good at it—in my opinion—but I have a purpose outside of protecting people."

"Me too! I love sports. I'm great at footy and all kinds of other things. I'm also the fastest," Marcus says as he grips the arm of the chair and leans closer to Charlotte, waggling his eyebrows.

"We have other hobbies and passions, of course. We have all the free will and consciousness of any person, mortal or otherwise," I say, giving Atlas a sharp look as he begins to open his mouth.

The young gargoyle chuffs and shakes his head, tipping his body back before slinking out into the hall.

Eloise steps back into the room with two large boxes of pizza.

"I assume this is what you were expecting when I arrived?" She keeps her words directed at Charlotte and moves past me and my nest-mates like we're a part of the furniture. She puts the boxes onto Charlotte's lap. "My job seems to be done. Text me if you need anything."

Eloise leaves with a nod to each of us and an additional warning look toward Atlas.

The younger witch takes a deep breath, her eyelids fluttering closed as she takes in the smell of pizza. Her stomach gives another thunderous growl before she pops open the top box and fishes out a slice with strange meat on it.

"I can't believe he was really able to get Canadian bacon." She takes a big bite and moans.

The sound strikes me in the core, and I stiffen. Beside me, Julius goes rigid as well, and Marcus nearly swoons. His eyes practically form hearts as he gazes at the witch.

"How long will you be staying?" My voice is tight, her soft sounds of pleasure a siren's song to my cock.

Charlotte swallows, dabbing her lips with a napkin that was in the box, and she shrugs. "I'm hoping to get the whole finding myself requirement done quickly. I'm hoping to keep it under a year."

Clearing my throat, I take a step back, toward what I hope is the door.

"We'll leave you to your pizza. Let us know if you have any other questions. We'll be around but stay out of your hair for the most part. Are you certain you only require a year?"

Marcus pouts hard as Charlotte nods, her mouth so full of pizza that it makes her cheeks puff. My mind drifts for a moment to what she might look like with my cock stuffed in her mouth. I clench my hands into fists and lengthen my claws to dig into my flesh.

I've never been so careless with my thoughts to let one interaction turn me into a sexual deviant.

"Should be all I need. I don't want to inconvenience you guys any more than I already have." Her eyes find Atlas, who stepped back into the room and is still brooding. "How hard can it be to find yourself?" she asks with an exasperated sigh.

I flee the room with a nod, wondering the same thing.

JULIUS

Darius leaves the room without another word, but I can't find it in myself to pull away from this woman just yet. Charlotte. Her name is Charlotte, and it fits her sort of perfectly.

"Mind if we stay?" I ask, trying to keep my tone casual.

"I'm out," Atlas says bluntly, casting one more burning look at Charlotte before he follows our alpha from the room.

"Well, may Marcus and I stay?" I rephrase my question.

Charlotte seems to glitch, a little scrunch pulling her face and a twitch jerking her forward a touch. She holds up a finger, swallowing her mouthful of pizza before she smiles. "Of course, it's your house—uh, castle."

"It's our castle for sure, but mi castle es tu castle, am I right?" Marcus chuckles.

Charlotte sets her pretty eyes on me for further explanation, and I bite my cheek to suppress my grin. I remove my glasses and lift the corner of my sweater, using the improper material to clean the glass. Her eyes flick down, following the move, and her gaze almost heats my skin.

There might be something more to this witch than even Marcus first gleaned. My sporty nest-mate has always been the most open to changes in our environment and magic, but even I can't deny the *something* that is there with Charlotte near.

"So the big blue gargoyle is the owner of the castle?" she asks, taking a small bite of her slice.

"That's right. We lost the deed about a hundred years ago.

Things get misplaced in magical spaces and then never turn up—"
I begin.

"Or they turn up attached to a very pretty witch," Marcus
chimes in.

Charlotte blushes and shakes her head. "Thanks, but it's not
exactly attached to me, per se. I thought this castle belonged to my
aunt?"

I wince slightly, shrugging to hide the movement. "It's impossible. We've been the only owners since the castle was built. We've
also been the only occupants."

Charlotte purses her pretty pink mouth as she takes in that
information.

"So I'm going to find out jack about my family here?" Her
cute little nose scrunches up from displeasure.

I bite into my lower lip, fighting the urge to press my mouth
across the bridge of her nose.

"Not necessarily," Marcus says suddenly, one hand flying to
rest on her knee. "If they ever lived in town, then Eloise will help
you find info."

"Speaking of her, um, why was she so...willing to go along with
this ownership stuff?" she asks.

Her intelligence is nearly giving me a hard-on.

"Eloise knows better than most to roll with the punches when
it comes to weird magic shit," Marcus says with a scoff. "Plus,
Darius said it was OK, and we sorta need the actual deed back."

"Right," she murmurs. "Right, right, OK, so...I can stay?"

"This is technically your castle now, but of course you can
stay," I say. "Darius did agree to a year, and I'm sure that could be
extended if you needed."

*Or wanted. Forever seems like just enough time to stay and find
yourself.*

"Talking about the castle and our alpha sure is a gas," Marcus
snorts. "So can I ask you about *you* now? And may I have a slice?"
he asks, giving her knees a squeeze, and her cheeks go crimson.

"I order too much anyway." She pushes some hair behind her ear. "Since we're going to be living together, I'm an open book, ask away," she says as she rests her hand on top of Marcus'.

My breath catches in my throat at how perfect they look together before Marcus shuffles forward and grabs a slice of pizza with his mouth from her lap.

CHAPTER 11

CHARLOTTE

I DON'T KNOW how I'm going to tell my sister that I spent my night chatting with some hot gargoyles and eating surprisingly good pizza. She's going to kick my ass, then kill me, cry about my death, find a way to bring me back, and then throttle me for not giving her an impossible invite to the fun.

I feel like I'm more lost than when I began. Maybe going through the whole cycle of life and death at the hands of my best friend would help me get out of my head for a bit.

They're all so stinking hot that I can't think like a rational and logical person, but I need to. There's no way I can resist literally carved-to-perfection men. Add in the fact they have tails and wings, and it alights something in my fantasy reader heart and loins.

We're going to be roommates—castle-mates, really—and they're just supernaturally beautiful in different ways. Cool, cool, cool. I can totally handle that. I'm pretty but not supernaturally *hot* like them.

I groan and toss myself onto the bed I've laid claim to, shuffling under the blankets without so much as dressing after my incredible shower. I don't have the mental energy to deal, so I shall not. Nothing wrong with being naked in my own castle...but not my own anymore.

"I am so fucked," I groan, pressing my face deeper into the pillow like maybe it's a portal to Narnia but a Narnia where things are normal again. So normal-er?

I snicker at my silly joke, tossing and turning until the bed is the perfect amount of messed up before I grab my phone from the nightstand. It's a decently acceptable time to be calling across the ocean right now, but the fear around my throat hasn't released its iron grip. I want to tell her everything and nothing because right now these gargoyles are mine. Something about keeping them my dirty little secret feels thrilling.

"Mine?" Saying the word out loud makes it feel even more ridiculous. "They are so not mine."

My finger hovers over the call button on her contact, but I can't find the strength, or the will, to get over myself, just yet.

I toss my phone into the mess of sheets and blankets and stare at the ceiling. A gargoyle now lives right above me. His office is right next to me too. Marcus is down the hall with Julius. And Atlas...I have no clue where he is, but I think that's for the best.

When he was in the room with me, I felt like my skin was on fire. Everything about the way he looked at me made me want to fight him and then fuck him. I've never had such a strong feeling about anything except my art, and even that's pushing it.

"I'm just getting used to it. It's been a while since I've done the deed, and now I'm just wondering what gargoyle dicks look like," I grumble as I drift my hand under the covers.

I take my time, appreciating every bit of soft skin that my body has to offer. The lumps, bumps, and rolls may not be for everyone, but I know I'm fucking beautiful because of them and not despite them. I give one of my breasts a hard squeeze, trying to imagine what it would feel like if my grip were replaced with one of stone.

My breath catches as my other hand, almost without conscious thought, delves right between my plush thighs and parts my dripping folds. I'm already throbbing, and I haven't even thought about anything penetrating me. Just looking at them all, I'm sure I could come absolute buckets if this is the reaction my body is having.

"Holy fuck—" I hiss as my fingertips make contact with my throbbing clit, and I nearly come from the simple contact.

My vision is filled with blinding stars as I bite hard into my lip to keep from embarrassing myself.

Slowly, when I'm sure I'm about to combust, I begin to circle my clit with the pads of two fingers, rolling the sensitive little bundle in the way I like best. I slowed my breathing to longer, softer moans as I pinch and pull at my nipple in time with the lazy circles. It feels so damn good to make love to myself after everything.

I'm not the same person I was when I stepped foot onto that plane in America. When I got off that plane, the world was different and I was sprinting to catch up. Now I'm just here, and I'm enjoying myself. The pizza was good, the conversation with Julius and Marcus was even better, and this...well, this is going to be cataclysmically amazing.

I whimper, turning my face toward the window, forcing my eyes wide to stave off the orgasm that is barrelling toward me. On either side of me are hot, strong men who are undoubtedly skilled in the ways of the female orgasm. There's no way you get to be that fucking sexy without being baptized in a woman's cum.

The thought of all of them, mouths and fingers soaked with my release, is what sends me barreling over the edge. My legs lock, and my whole body spasms with the force of the orgasm that nearly makes me squirt.

"Marcus!" I cry his name quietly before ripping my hand away from my breast and slapping it over my mouth.

For a long moment I hold my breath, not moving a muscle,

and just wait. I should have asked if they have super hearing, or if the walls of the castle were thick enough to withstand some pent-up woman's clitoral DJ session. Now I feel like a fucking pervert. He was so sweet to me, and all I want to do is rail him while he prattles on about his beloved footie.

"Footie." I snort a little. "He means soccer."

The next morning comes far too quickly. A lot like me last night.

I groan as my body involuntarily stretches out and pulls at all the taut muscles I must have used to have the best orgasm of my life last night.

"Fuck, ouch." I try to complain, but my mouth is so dry that my tongue is sticking to the roof of it. "Water, breakfast, need."

Rolling out of bed is a Herculean effort, but I manage it and even get myself into a pair of overalls and a T-shirt before I walk out stark naked. What a way to greet the day and my new room-mates, with my tits just...right there.

I shuffle out of my room with my eyes basically closed and find my way to the kitchen on the ground floor. The room is warm and smells of baking bread, but as I tiptoe around, I find where the scent and sounds of life are actually coming from. Tucked into the corner is a small, nondescript staircase. Taking it down a few steps brings me into an even larger and more castle-chic commercial-style kitchen.

Julius stands before one of the three different stove tops, stirring a pot. Freshly baked loaves of bread and muffins sit steaming on the counter.

My mouth waters at the smell of citrus and sweetness, so I follow my nose right to the muffins. I lick my lips, not having alerted Julius to my presence yet, as I slowly scoop one up. I didn't notice that none of the muffins have liners until I'm holding a steaming hot breakfast pastry in my hand.

"Hot!" I yelp, dropping the poor muffin to the floor and shaking out my reddening hand.

Julius is beside me in a second, cradling my hand in both of his, the tips of his fingers brushing gently over the skin as he looks at the injury.

"Nothing permanent or life threatening, thankfully. Maybe grab a plate next time." He chuckles softly but doesn't let go of my hands as he looks down at me. "Want a muffin? Or was it just the thrill of the pilfering that gets you going?"

My face goes more crimson than my smarting hand. "No! Nothing gets me going. I'm not a pervert."

The green gargoyle laughs again, and I notice his wings are gone, along with his tail, and he isn't actually all that green anymore. Instead, he has human-like skin, and he's tan, as if he spent a few hours soaking up the sun on a beach. His hair is soft looking and warm brown with a slight wave to it, but he still has verdant green horns. I force myself not to look at his perfect mouth. I did way too much of that while he was telling me about his love of cooking last night.

"What happened to your—" I point at him, snapping my mouth shut so I don't offend him any more than I probably have already.

I need to get food and water and hide in my art room for the rest of eternity, or however long it takes to discover myself, whichever is longer.

He smiles and pushes up the gold frames of his cool octagonal glasses. "It's a bit of magic. We can...be more or less of our supernatural selves at will. This is like...twenty-five percent," he says and tips his head in thought, his horns catching the light and sparkling brilliantly.

"Do you have gems in your horns?" I can't help the question.

I was talking to this guy for a few hours last night before going to bed, and I didn't notice just how truly spectacular he is to look at. Silly me. Spank bank has been updated.

"Yes, I installed them myself." He reaches up and touches the base absentmindedly.

My jaw drops. *Installed them.*

The pot on the stove bubbles up angrily, hissing steam and making him curse.

"Sorry, simmer pots like to be tended." He returns to his place and begins to stir the pot gently, coaxing it back to an actual simmer.

"This is really weird."

"What is?" Julius asks, keeping his eyes on the pot.

"Everything, but mostly the fact that magic is real, and this castle is magic, and you're magic."

"I think it's a beautiful thing, not a weird thing." He teases me so easily, the grin on his face taking any sting from the words before it can even land.

"Beautiful, sure, you're beautiful, but—" I pause. "Wait."

"Why, thank you, Charlotte. I think you are very beautiful yourself," he says, and the dark little chuckle that follows makes me shiver, my nipples getting hard as fucking diamonds.

"Thank you. I just keep making this more and more awkward, don't I?" I deflate as the words tumble out.

"No, not really. You're sweet. Here, take this and serve yourself a muffin with the tongs. Have a nice slice of bread if you like. Butter is in the fridge and jam is in the pantry." He offers me a plate with his non-stirring hand.

I take the plate wordlessly and do as the gargoyle says. I give myself another muffin and a thick slice of bread, slathering it in cold butter that melts almost instantly and then jam. As I leave the kitchen, I try not to think about where the dropped muffin disappeared to.

My makeshift art studio is quiet in the early afternoon light. My empty breakfast plate sits licked clean on the small *"paint-free zone"* table beside me. The muffin that Julius made was the best I've ever had. Two points to Ireland. One for their muffins. And another one to their orgasms. Maybe that's why all I can think about is painting pastries with thick white glaze.

I flick the brush across the canvas, adding a softer white for a highlight, and sit back on the stool I stole from the kitchen when I first moved in.

I never paint still-life paintings, but now that's all I can conjure. Moments and things that don't quite exist yet. I want to capture them and sink my teeth right in.

Fighting off the urge to get a new canvas and paint the creator of such fine muffins, I mix up a vivid sky blue instead.

The weather has remained a terrible mess, the clouds thick and dark, promising heavy rains in the near future. I want to remember the few perfect moments of unreality when I got here. The sun was too yellow for the dreary bruised sky, the grass too green...a lot like a certain gargoyle—a few of them.

I groan a little and set the palette of paints aside, trying to refrain from mixing the base tones of their skin and just make anything else. I'm more than capable of making lots of "elses," but my mind does not want "elses"—it wants them.

"I'm going to lose my marbles if I can't paint." I huff, standing up and pacing in front of the huge windows with incredible views of the loch on one side and the path toward the town on the other.

Of course I chose the armory as my painting room. It was a mostly empty room when I found it, but I can see it returned to all its glory in my mind's eye. Swords and shields hang from the walls, and big suits of armor are positioned to look like someone is inside, ready to protect you.

"Charlotte, there you are!" Marcus' bright voice brings me back to the present.

A jolt of awareness of him snaps against my skin.

He smiles widely at me, standing at the mouth of my converted painting room, holding up a soccer ball in one hand. "Care to come out and watch me kick this around for a bit before the weather turns?"

"Um." I glance out the window again. It could rain any minute, and I'm hestitent to be the reason he can't enjoy the slight break in shit weather. "Sure, that sounds fun."

"Sweet." He tosses the ball up and catches it in his horns.

The space between them is just wide enough for the ball to perch against the body of his horns, long and straight before they come to an abruptly tapered end that points straight up. It's almost like a *Z* if you start from where they meet his hairline.

"I take it you'll be showing off the entire time?"

"Of course I will. There is a pretty bird watching me." He shoots me a wink, and I can't help but blush.

I've never been called a bird before, but the slang will grow on me, as well as the accents…I hope. If I'm going to be staying here for at least a year, integrating with these gargoyles, then I need to get used to the Irish verbiage.

"Alright, let's go so you can kick that soccer ball around."

Marcus scoffs, hopping up and sending the ball into the air before catching it again. "Football, Char, it's a football."

Never trust the weather in the Irish countryside. The lesson is now bone deep, along with the chill.

"I'm so sorry, Charlotte. I thought we had a right bit more time than that," Marcus says, gripping the huge fluffy towel he had been drying me off with.

"It's OK, it's just so cold. Is it normally that cold?" I ask, teeth starting to chatter slightly as I sit on the bottom of the steps that lead to the second floor.

"I mean, I can't entirely feel it," he says as he goes about drying the ends of my hair with a delicacy that makes me melt. "With the stone skin and all, temperature doesn't really play a factor in my comfort. You have to let me know before it gets this bad next time. I wouldn't be a very good protector if you got sick on my watch."

He suddenly sits behind me, the towel between us. He takes one of my hands and gives it the slightest squeeze, like he's afraid to break me. The difference in our heights is something I've been trying to ignore. I'm not used to feeling small. All the guys make me feel small in a good way, and that's only beginning to lead toward unnecessary feelings.

I feel cared for and precious and delicate. I've never let anyone get this close before.

I swallow thickly, trying not to let on how damn comfortable he feels. I want so badly to steal all of him for myself. "You feel warm to me."

"Magic. I need to think about it a little when I want to be warm. Otherwise I'm just sorta...room temperature?" He tips his head and squints at the thought. "Oh god, I must feel like a dead body."

I snort loudly, my hand snapping up to catch the last bit of sound before I gaze up at him. God, Marcus doesn't seem like he would go all monster on me if I offend him, but it's the last thing I want to do. He's been so sweet.

"I doubt you feel dead. Besides, when would you have the time to...be felt like that?"

I'm slowly shoving my foot into my mouth, but I can't stop myself. I can feel my heart beating in my throat, my pulse racing and blood pumping. I'm curious if these guys fuck, because maybe they don't. If they've all taken a vow of celibacy to protect mortals, it would be the second saddest day of my life.

"That's a very naughty thing to ask, Char." He teases me, bending his head down toward mine.

Fuck, it's already too late. I realize that as Marcus leans down and captures my lips with his, or did I lean up and kiss him? It's hard to tell once I fall right into the delight of having his mouth on mine. He's so fucking warm, and he tastes clean and fresh. His mouth is surprisingly soft but with a little firmness, like a tensed muscle.

He wraps his arms around my waist and lifts me into his lap. Our soaked clothes are plastered to our bodies, and I can't find it in me to complain about what I'm feeling through the fabric. I've never liked being poked by an erection before, but there's a first time for everything, I guess.

His chest is as hard and chiseled as stone, and it makes me giggle against his lips. He takes that as an invitation to slide his tongue into my mouth, and my brain short-circuits. It's just a regular tongue that this very hot supernatural man is shoving into my mouth. I moan around it and begin to suck, doing my best to press my breasts against him and be sexy. But, of course, I'm wearing gross, soggy overalls, and as I try to rock myself against him, the wet denim starts to chafe my thighs.

"That feels so weird," I murmur and pull back.

"What? Me? Oh my gosh, I'm so sorry, I've never done it with a witch before." He rambles, quickly removing me from his lap and placing me back on the stairs. He kneels at my feet on the floor. "I'm so sorry. I can go less gargoyle if you want."

My jaw drops as a lot of information flies at me all at once. Each point lands like a dart on a board, but the most important of all: Me? A witch?

"Did you just call me a witch?"

CHAPTER 12

CHARLOTTE

"Uh, yes?" Marcus says with an adorably confused look on his face. His thick brows knit together like he's trying to do mental math as he mutters, "Do you prefer the term sorceress or wizard or something? I've never really interacted with any magic users besides Eloise and my nest-mates."

My mind is spinning, trying to grasp onto something other than this conversation. The sensations in my body, how amazingly turned on I was just a minute ago, before some life-changing bull-shit came out of Marcus' mouth.

"Please stop talking," I whisper.

Marcus' mouth snaps shut, the click of his teeth soft in comparison to the pounding of my heart.

Everything feels both numb and tingling. Pins and needles race up and down my arms and legs, and my fingers ache straight to the bone and not from the cold.

"This was a bad idea," I say. "We shouldn't have done that. You're...well, you're..."

The word I'm looking for doesn't exist in my vocabulary. How can '*so fucking perfect for me in such a short time that it makes me want to forget everything Kennedy taught me about being a good slut and just be a bad one*' be boiled down to a single word?

"I'm what?" Marcus tips his chin up, though his bottom lip quivers like he's about to cry.

His eyes go a little glassy, and for the first time tonight, I notice how beautiful they look. He's a warm yellow, all bright and as sunshiny as he is on the inside, but his eyes? They're the most perfect shade of brown.

"Marcus! I need some help with this pot!"

Julius' voice seems to come from nowhere and startles the hell out of me.

Marcus stands and gives me a begrudging half smile. "Finish this talk later?" he asks.

Though before I can answer, he's gone in a blur of yellow.

I can't help the little laugh that bubbles out from between my lips. "I knew it wasn't a ghost."

"I'm not a witch. I can't be a witch. He's wrong," I grumble when I get back to my room, pacing back and forth on the plush carpet while trying not to lose the collective rest of my own marbles. "I need to call Kennedy, I need to..."

I grab my phone and open her contact, staring for a minute too long at the picture of us from our college days. It was Halloween, either our sophomore or junior year, but at that point, we weren't interested in candy. Booze had a bigger appeal, so we wore the same costumes all four years and got blitzed out of our minds. It was the best and worst of times. I still can't stomach tequila.

I hold the phone to my ear as it rings once, twice, three times before going to voicemail. My shoulders slump as something inside me withers. I'm being overdramatic, but everything feels like it's falling apart now, and she's the only one who can help me keep it together.

I bring my fingers to my mouth and nip at my nails, ripping at the skin around my nail beds. The sharp taste of copper fills my mouth as blood begins to weep from the small wounds. I can't help but roll my tongue around them to lap up the blood, even if it isn't the cleanest of habits. I grip my phone in my other hand, heart jumping into my throat as it chimes.

"Not a call," I grunt in frustration as I debate chucking my phone out the window and into the loch.

The thought feels good for a second before settling into something akin to cement in my belly.

I don't even bother to check the text right now. I need her voice to soothe me, and texting will only make this worse.

Tossing my phone onto the bed, I shake my head and head out of my room.

"I need something. Maybe snacks, maybe booze, maybe to rub it out." I shuffle toward the kitchen, keeping my eyes glued to the floorboards, up until I smack into a wall that I don't remember being in the middle of the hall.

"Ouch. Watch yourself, pest," the wall hisses.

OK, definitely not a wall.

"Hey!" I snap, my head jerking up until I can lock eyes with those of the dusky gargoyle. Atlas stands far too tall above me, but I pull my shoulders back and puff out my chest. "I was clearly walking somewhere with my head down."

"Who does that?" he asks with a scoff before dusting off the front of his plain white T-shirt as if I sullied it by bumping into him. "You need to mind yourself. This isn't your home."

I know it isn't. My home is across the damn ocean, but I don't back down.

"If that's the case, then show me your deed," I say with a smirk.

Atlas's jaw tenses, and I can hear his teeth grind from his agitation. "You are a nuisance, pest. Keep out of my way until you're gone."

He slinks down the hall around me, his tail whipping like an agitated cat as he goes.

I can't help it when I look after him and flip him double birds. He deserves it. I don't really want to be here, but I need to. This place was somehow willed to me, and I don't get any of the money that was left to me without being here for at least a bit.

"At least he didn't call me a witch." I shake my head, the anger boiling inside me making it hard to continue.

I curl my toes against the floor, and I have to clench my hands into fists to keep from peeling off more skin from my fingers.

"I'm not a witch, and I'm not a pest." I force a laugh. "But that's a new one."

I end up wandering aimlessly around the castle, stomping like a petulant child. I want to stake some kind of claim on the space that felt like mine and not mine in equal measure.

When I'm finally calm, I find myself upstairs in front of a door left ajar with noise spilling out. It's not a bad noise, so I take a chance and peek in.

Darius, the biggest gargoyle, sits behind a desk made to fit him, with his head tipped toward a laptop. The room is dimly lit by candles, so his light blue face is cast in hard shadows from the glow of the screen.

"I can feel you watching me, Charlotte. Come in."

"I should have known better than to just...lurk."

"Everyone deserves to lurk, but I am too preoccupied to endure any staring." He leans back in his chair and gives a heavy sigh.

"You sound like the weight of the world is on your shoulders."

"No, it's not the entire world, but a good chunk of it. We have to go back to more blatant protection." His eyes drift to a map on the far wall. A large chunk of Europe is circled, in addition to Ireland "Before, when all supernaturals were a part of the environment of the mortal world, we played an active role in things like diplomacy and protection from natural disasters and other supernaturals. But there was a change in thought among mortals and we were all dangerous, we were forced to hide ourselves, so we shifted gears instead."

"How so?" I step more into his office.

The heavy scent of old pages and leather fills my nose as I come to stand before his desk. I wish I could see this space with the light on, see exactly what he's hiding in here that I can poke around in. We have electricity now, but this seemingly broody gargoyle is only illuminated by his laptop screen.

"Virtual protection as well as hiring human mercenaries and such. Little things to keep my mind occupied while the others were able to indulge in their passions," he says with a dismissive wave toward his laptop.

"So you've still been protecting people, just without them knowing? Are you guys rich?" I ask, suddenly wondering where all the money I'm supposed to get will be coming from.

Darius leans back farther, letting his head loll back against the leather chair. It's similar to the one in the sitting room, but this one looks less comfortable. He arches a brow at me, and I'm startled as I watch his skin drain of that stark blue color and take on a very human olive complexion. His hair and horns change in a blink; his hair goes from blue to a rich brown, and his horns vanish completely as if they were never there.

"It's not impossible for us to blend in, so yes, we protected humanity without them knowing," he says casually, something changing in his demeanor. His eyelids droop slightly, and a confident but lazy smile tugs at his lips. It's so unfair how, despite transforming out of his stone form, he keeps his chiseled cheeks and jaw. "I don't normally deposit and tell, but we would be very embarrassing immortals if we were *not* rich."

"I guess so," I blurt, going instantly red in the face.

His dark eyes run over me in a way that I can damn near feel. I suddenly want to lean on the desk and beg him to fuck me. Something about his air makes me want to let him ruin me.

"I think I can see why you're the alpha of the...nest." I squeak out the words, the red in my face crawling down my neck and up to the tips of my ears.

"Is that right?" he asks with a chuckle as he leans forward, his fingers interlaced and his elbows resting on the desk.

Those fathomless eyes bore right into my damn soul.

Holy shit. When did the sleeves of his button-down shirt get rolled up to his elbows? It should be illegal for a man made of stone most of the time to have that many thick veins. I'm nearly salivating over them as I run my eyes over each one before finding his face again.

He grins at me, knowing exactly what I was doing. Eyeing him up like the sexy piece of man meat he undoubtedly is.

Man meat. I've never thought that in my life, but here I am, practically panting over this near stranger.

"Any more interesting questions, Charlotte?"

I'm tempted to either blurt out something stupid and nonsensical or just run, but instead, I take another step into his office and then another until I get to his desk. Then I perch one cheek of my bountiful ass on the edge.

"Can I watch you work for a while? I'm not in the headspace to paint, Marcus and I—"

"What did he do?" Darius asks, shooting from his chair quicker than it takes me to blink.

"Nothing! Nothing. He's been so sweet, and we kissed...OK, we kissed." I sigh, trying not to let the truth slip into my expression.

We did more than share the most perfect kiss I've ever had, then he called me a witch, and now the world is flipped all over again.

Darius' hands are blue again, nails turned to sharp claws that dig deep gouges into the surface of his desk. I suck in a sharp breath, and his eyes follow mine, locked onto his claws. He jerks his hands back and stuffs them into the pockets of his well-tailored slacks. His tail makes an appearance, giving an almost apologetic sway.

"I see. You wanted to kiss him?" he asks, tone taking on a deep, rich tone that makes something inside me sigh.

"Yes, very much so. He showed off a little by playing football, and then it started raining. He brought me inside, and it happened. It was amazing," I say, like I need to calm Darius down.

They have some weird magical connection, so who knows, maybe Darius can smite Marcus from here.

"Very well," he says, sliding back into his seat and adjusting his laptop on his desk so I can see the screen.

Well, mostly see it. I shimmy on his desk, propping the other ass cheek on it, and glance at all the numbers on spreadsheets, live maps sending out pings, and chat boxes rolling with numbers and text that's probably words but scroll by far too fast for me to read them.

"How do you not have the world's biggest headache?"

"I live with Marcus and Atlas. I deal with them both constantly and have for hundreds of years. Spreadsheets are nothing in comparison."

The next morning I feel too good for everything that happened yesterday to be a fever dream. I yawn big and stretch out in my bed, my tongue rolling around in my mouth to taste for any leftover traces of alcohol. Nothing. Everything that took place yesterday really happened, and it was...interesting.

"Witch stuff. Gotta do...witch research," I groan.

Tipping my head toward the open window, I try to coax myself from the tangle of warm sheets but find that my eyelids are just too heavy. Whatever I was dreaming about was too comforting for me to leave just yet. A soft sigh slips from my lips as I pull the covers over my head.

The moment of peace is shattered into a million pieces when my phone rings.

I shove my hand under the edge of the blanket and grope around on my nightstand until I find my phone and reel it back in. Kennedy's name flashes on the screen along with the picture of us. I do the math in my head, trying to count back the hours to see what time it is in New York before I pick up.

"Hello?"

"Bitch, you took forever to answer!" she squeals, her voice dripping with excitement.

"Sorry, I was asleep, like you should be. It's just normal for someone on this side of the world to be awake. What's your excuse?"

"I went to bone town!"

I groan, shoving my head back into my pillow. "Please tell me you didn't go back and fuck Chad."

"Hell, no, I didn't. You really think I'd climb back into bed with him when there are monsters lurking?" She giggles at me like we're sharing a secret.

Oh, she has no idea.

"So, you met a monster...person," I begin, waiting for her to fill in the juicy details.

"I did, and they were...well, a little bit unexpected. I have no clue what they were, but my god."

"Gods," I whisper reflexively.

"Sure, yeah, gods, they were something. Thin as a rail and sorta

93

nerdy but so damn sweet! They took me to dinner downtown, and then we went to see that new documentary on the deep sea. It scared the shit out of me, so they took me home early, and we got it the fuck on." She sighs like we're back in high school again and she finally got the attention of the entire football team.

"I see, so things went well, and you're skipping the gory details —thank you, by the way—because?"

"Well, I can't exactly kiss and tell when I want to see them again." Her tone is so matter of fact that I laugh.

I laugh so hard that tears begin to stream down my face. One thing my sister never does is see hookups again who she actually likes. Something in her DNA just repels actual romantic feelings.

"You bitch, shut uuuuup," she whines, drawing out the words.

I swear I can hear her stomp her foot in the background, too, but I'm unsure as my breath comes in steady hiccups.

"OK— Sorry— Trying," I gasp, my stomach muscles twinging with pain from laughing.

"I mean it! I'm going to see him again. He's really sweet, and before I left, he gave me his prized possession."

"Their nuts?" I ask with a snort.

"No, a limited edition Color-Fighters lunch box," she practically purrs.

It's really odd that she's preening over a lunch box inspired by an early 2000s kids' show.

My mouth snaps shut, and I think I stop breathing. This is so fucking weird. Either that or my sister was body snatched.

"What? Lottie? Lottie, you there?" she asks after what feels like the longest two minutes of my life.

"You're in love." The awe dripping from my words makes her sniff on the other end of the line.

"Am not. I'm finally letting a man treat me the way I'm supposed to be treated," she says, and I can hear her signature pout.

"Sure, of course, you're totally doing that and not just...in insta-love with this random nerd."

"I am not in love. You know I don't do love and won't until I stop fitting into my skinny jeans," she grumbles.

"Doubt that will happen, Kenn, but I don't doubt that something is going on with this nice nerd of yours. I'm happy for you," I say softly.

She sighs again, all the tension leaving her body through that exhalation of breath. "I am too. It's nice to feel like a person for once."

"You're always a person, too good of a person for anyone, especially some finance bro named Chad."

She scoffs. "I'm basically your finance bro."

"You wish. You don't have a bro bone in your body."

"I certainly did last night..." she singongs.

"I'm hanging up now," I hiss, clicking the end-call button as she cackles. "And they think I'm the witch."

CHAPTER 13

CHARLOTTE

"Julius, hey," I say, trying to stop myself from running into him in my haste to get into the kitchen and eat something.

My feet trip over some of the cobblestones in the floor, and the green gargoyle gently rests a hand on my upper arm to steady me.

"Hello to you too, Charlotte. I was actually about to bring this up to you." He flicks his eyes upward to his other hand, holding a plate that wafts steam toward the beams in the ceiling.

"Really?" My jaw drops a little.

"Of course, what better way to get on the good side of your new roommate than to ply her with breakfast?" he asks with a teasing smile as he lowers the plate in front of my face.

It's stacked with a pile of fluffy scrambled eggs studded with peppers, a hunk of fresh crusty bread, bacon glistening with grease, and a wedge of melon covered in itty bitty fresh berries.

"This looks incredible."

"Well, I thought about a full English and decided instead to do a full Irish...well, a full Irish, Julius style."

"Can I sit in here?"

The formal dining room is huge, meant for an army instead of a lone artist, and has way too much space. The subterranean part of the kitchen is much cozier.

"Of course. Mind if we break our fasts together?" He sets my plate down on the island next to a cup of hot coffee with cream and a bowl of plain yogurt.

"I didn't know gargoyles needed to eat," I say as I nod, sliding into the seat.

I'm far too entranced by the breakfast offerings to be overly polite or even embarrassed about the literal drool beading on my bottom lip.

"We don't need to, but it's nice. We appreciate food like mortals do but don't gain anything from it overly so," Julius says as he slides into the seat beside me.

He pulls another plate in front of himself and dishes large portions of the same foods he served me onto his plate.

"So you just...eat it, and it goes nowhere?" I ask and shove both a strip of bacon and a berry into my mouth at the same time.

A groan slips out of me at how fucking good they taste together. The berry is so tart and sweet, while the bacon adds a richness and a bite of salt.

I chew my bite before I glance at Julius, who is staring at me from behind the rims of those gold glasses. His lips are parted like I've caught the very breath from his lungs, and his pupils are blown wide. I flush, licking my lips, trying to tuck in my stomach but failing miserably. He's probably staring at me because he's wondering why I'm shoving food into my mouth like I haven't eaten in months. But he's been nothing but kind. He's never looked at me funny before.

I flinch slightly, the sting of my own thoughts no less sharp just because I'm the one judging me. "Sorry, you make good food."

The apology is what seems to break the spell. He blinks, and his mouth snaps shut.

"No apology necessary. It's an honor to cook for you." The

wings behind him freeze, flexing before they ruffle themselves. They're large and bat-like but have gentle movements when they want to. "I mean, it's really nice to cook for someone who actually needs food to survive. Helps me to...try new things."

He picks up a small spoon and scoops a bit of the yogurt from his own small dish. Julius brings the spoon to his lips, and instead of taking it into his mouth, his tongue darts out and licks the creamy substance from the spoon. That clever tongue rolls around the silver utensil, making my traitorous nipples tighten.

"Enjoying it?" His lips are moving, the words are coming out, but that movement of his tongue on the spoon keeps replaying in my mind.

"Yes," I whisper. "I'm enjoying it very much."

"Good to know." He shifts his chair closer to mine. "Would it be OK if I ask you a few things? You've got me curious."

"Me? Made you curious?" I say, breathless.

"Insatiably so, if I'm being honest. I've stayed up late mulling over all the things I want to ask you." Angling his head down so he can catch my eyes more easily, he offers a warming smile.

"Fire away then." I beam in response.

I can deal with a little positive attention from a handsome monster. I am worthy of it.

"What brought you to Ireland? Besides inheriting the deed to the castle? Interested in the countryside?"

I bite my lip, shame flushing my cheeks as I shake my head. "Nope, I'm sorta shallow, I guess. I came to see the castle and qualify to get my inheritance."

"Qualify? Are there hidden stipulations or something?" he asks, and that sentence makes the Irish brogue in his voice thicker.

Something about it soothes me as it makes me think. "Not really hidden. They were right on the will in black and white. I never met the aunt I inherited this all from, so I was really surprised." I laugh softly, forcing the sound out because that's just what I do when things are painfully awkward inside my head.

"Your parents never told you? No trips with them when you were little? If you inherited the castle, then you must have ties to Ireland."

I wince sharply, nearly falling off my seat if not for Julius. With his tail, he catches the chair before it tips, and he wraps his hands around my waist to keep me from moving an inch. I want to claw into him and make him release me so I can run and never look back at this beautiful kitchen and the handsome gargoyle.

It feels like he's lit a match to start one of his simmer pots, but he doesn't know I've actually filled the whole pot with flammable gas.

"My parents are dead." The words are matter of fact, flat, even, to the ears of anyone who might expect heartbreak or deep sorrow.

He digs his fingers into my sides, grip tightening as I wiggle slightly. Some of my urges are harder to suppress than others, and the one to flee is nearly nuclear at the moment. Julius' expression softens, and he tips his chin down a little. His glasses scratch gently down his nose before he makes a soft *shhh* sound.

"I'm so sorry, Charlotte. Just breathe, you're alright. I won't hurt you," he whispers, hands not budging, though his tail drifts up and pushes my hair back from my face.

The thought of biting him quickly passes through my mind, and it rips a laugh from me that borders on hysterical. Then, the tears that I didn't know had been building roll down my cheeks.

"I'm so fucking sorry," he repeats, pulling me easily from my stool and into his lap, crushing me in a hug that constricts my breaths but imparts a heavy feeling of security.

"I was in high school, but it"—*hiccup*—"still sucks so much" —*hiccup*—"I never got to ask them so many questions, and then Marcus said something,"

"And what was that, sweetling?" Julius asks, moving one hand from around me to the middle of my back to rub soothing circles.

"He said I was a witch!" Even to my ears, the words sound more hysterical than my accompanying sob.

Julius stiffens but says nothing.

Tears and snot flood down my face, and surely, any illusion of possible attractiveness he might have felt toward me must fizzle and die a hard death.

"And why the fuck are you all so hot? It's like some kind of cosmic fuck you," I croak, the wave of emotion finally ebbing.

My hands must have been moving of their own volition because when I finally realize they're resting against his chest, I can feel steady warmth and pulsing beneath my fingertips. I hesitate to keep them there. But the heavy presence of Julius' hand on my back never lets up. As he continues to rub steady circles, it helps my breaths come more evenly.

When I can breathe without hiccupping, he speaks. "I see. I'm so sorry about your parents, Charlotte. You're here now, and if I can, I'll help you find all the answers you want."

I clench my hands into fists, the lack of straight answers winding my whole being tight.

"And the witch thing?" I murmur.

"I don't think I'm the best person to talk to you about that. Have you thought about talking to Eloise? She and her wife practice, and they would be much better help than any of my nest. We have some magic, but it's entirely different stuff," he explains gently. He cups my cheek with the hand not stroking my back and guides my face so we make eye contact. "But I do believe you're a witch and a special one at that."

I sniffle, leaning into his touch. "Great."

I think about contacting Eloise. I really, really, really think about it, but I talk myself out of it in the end. It feels like a lot to put on a kindly stranger, even if she is a witch too. Instead, I do the only thing I can think of and turn to the internet. With supernaturals revealing themselves, there *has* to be a wealth of knowledge some-where. If anything, there have to at least be a few books that will hold more water than the stuff that populates some Reddit forums. I scroll through a forum on witchcraft for an hour before I realize that *no actual witches are probably in established covens* or whatever.

I shut my laptop with a groan.

I don't want to call Eloise, but I need to. She's the only one with any sort of information on this aunt of mine. I try to think of how I'm going to broach the subject.

Should I just come out with it and ask? Should I try to get her to bring up the big W word? Should I just try another day and do it in person?

"Fuck that idea," I breathe.

In-person questioning quickly gets pushed to the last resort section of my mental checklist.

Suddenly, my boobs begin to vibrate. My phone is stashed in there so I don't lose it when I'm wandering the castle. Slipping a hand into my overalls, under my shirt, and then into my bra, I peel my phone away from the flesh of my breast and wipe off some of the sweat with a wince.

"The humidity is no joke," I grumble as I look at the screen.

Eloise is calling.

"Son of a witch," I chuckle. "Hello?"

"Daughter of a witch, actually," she says around a yawn. "I was about to go to sleep with my wife when she kept divining that someone was in desperate need of a chat, and since everyone else in town knows that, after seven p.m., I spend time with my wife, I knew it must be you." She sounds exasperated, and I can't blame her.

I wasted the day with useless research when I should have just come to her instead of tiptoeing around it.

"I'm really sorry."

"No, that's not necessary, we're practically coven—" Another yawn steals the end of her words. "Just tell me what I can help you with so I can get some rest."

"Did I wake you?" I ask softly, biting at my nails.

"No, I was halfway to it on my wife's lap, but you caught us just in time. Now, enough of the waste-of-time questions. What do you really want to know?" Eloise asks, leaning into the word "want."

I swallow, lick my lips, bite at my nails, and think.

What's the real question I want to ask?

"It doesn't need to be 'What is the answer to the universe'—" She yawns again. "Maybe start with how you're a witch?"

"How am I a witch?" I squeak.

"Well, when a mommy witch and a daddy— Ouch, Dara, why did you whack me?" Eloise hisses softly.

"Stop being so grumpy. Answer the confused girl's questions, and be nice," an unfamiliar voice, who can only be Dara, says down the line.

"I'm always nice," Eloise grumbles. "Alright, you're a witch because one or both of your parents were witches. You need direct blood connection to inherit a line of magic. That or there has to be a binding contract signed by a divine body."

"And the castle? Does the bloodline come from Ireland? My aunt? What is a divine body?"

"Those are more nuanced questions, if I'm honest. I believe that the person who left you with the deed was in the same coven as your parents rather than a blood relation," she explains, her tone bordering on that you would use with a toddler. "As for divine bodies, think of it like this: from heaven, from hell, from the place in between that we cannot access without magic and a death wish."

"Got it." It's simple enough, even if it's scary as hell. "So I have magic?"

"You do indeed. My coven might be small"—I can hear a smile in her voice—"but I've got an eye for this stuff. You might be powerful, or you might have some eyes on you. Divine beings are right nosy bastards." She snickers.

There's a soft *thud* before Eloise laughs.

"A pillow, love, really?"

"Yes, hurry up. I'm your wife, and I desire snuggles."

Shuffling sounds over the line before their words become more muffled.

Biting my lip, I do my best to focus on other things. Like the swell of anxiety clawing its way up from the cheeks of my ass to the back of my throat. I want to vomit, and I want to chew my nails; I want to run away and scream, but I've got nowhere to go in Ireland but here.

"Excuse us, Charlotte. Eloise is being a tosser," Dara says with a lower chuckle over the phone.

Her voice is rich like a full-bodied wine, with a bite of sweetness.

"It's OK. I didn't realize you guys turn in so early. I'm a city girl who's used to insomnia," I say with a nervous laugh.

"What is your next question? I know a good deal about all this myself," she says, her voice laced with tenderness and an understanding of my confusion and hurt.

"Did you find out you were a witch later in your life too?" The question is barely a whisper. I'm surprised my phone even picks it up.

"I did." She pauses for a breath before continuing. "I was given up for adoption at birth, so there was a lot of learning to do. We can learn together, and Eloise will be our overly sarcastic professor." She teases the other woman with and undercurrent of admiration.

I want to just hang up so they can spend more time together, but I need a real plan.

"So, you'll both help me learn what it means to be a witch?" I ask softly, trying not to really hope, but this is all still so fucking weird.

It doesn't feel like my life at all. I just wanted some quiet self-contemplation to make some art in order to get my inheritance, but I guess this is the proverbial fine print of the situation.

"Of course. Come over tomorrow morning around nine, and we'll start with history," Dara says soothingly.

"OK, thank you. Thank you both so much."

"Good night, Charlotte," she says before ending the call.

My heart stalls in my chest, but all the fight has flooded out of me. This is enough for now. The promise of learning is enough.

When Dara said we would start with history, I didn't expect there to be this much. It's more intensive than any high school or college classes but only half as boring because of the use of magical runes to convey meaning. Learning from a book has never been my strong suit, but when it comes to the history of local covens, witches of note, and big magical events that happened over the last decade under the noses of mortals, I'm pretty dang good at remembering things.

"I believe your parents were a part of a coven that disbanded some time ago. There have been no other covens in the area—besides mine—for quite some time, and your aunt was not a member of mine." Eloise looks over an older map that Dara pulled from their attic.

Sitting across from the couple in their living room with all manner of papers and books spread out between us feels like we're on some sort of novice detective show. I've held myself back from cracking stupid quips about working hard and hardly working due to Eloise still being a little grumpy about last night.

"What causes a coven to disband? Why wouldn't my aunt go with my parents to America?" I ask, leaning over to try and read the map in the other witch's hands.

"A lot of things, deaths or disagreements, taxes and tariffs." Eloise scoffs. "Or simply just moving away and not keeping in contact."

"It doesn't happen often," Dara says, "because covens are close-knit groups for the most part and tend to be generational after their formation. Your aunt may have been from a different line but considered family due to the coven relationship."

"Your last name is Ryan, correct?" Eloise asks, setting down the map and grabbing a book bound in cherry-red leather.

"Yes, I kept it after the adoption," I murmur.

It was technically an adult adoption, so I filled out all my paperwork myself, but it didn't feel any less significant not to take my family's last name. I huff, trying not to let the internal guilt settle.

"Well, that's a fairly common Irish last name, so we've got our work cut out for us." She drops the book on the table with a thud, and the pages seem to furl out on their own, lengthening to the size of the coffee table and spilling over the edges. Hundreds of names fill the space, all with the same surname.

"Holy shit," I croak. My eyes feel strained, skipping from Ryan to Ryan as I try to fish my parents out of the sea of similar names. "Can't any of this be alphabetized?"

"Would you like to argue with the magical text about how they decide to organize their internals?" Eloise asks with a soft scowl that Dara responds to with a roll of her eyes.

"Most magical tomes don't just house magic but are magic. They often decide how the contents will be laid out," Dara explains, pushing a set of reading glasses up her nose.

I was stunned by her when we first officially met this morning. Her skin is the color of rain-soaked bark, her smile warm and inviting. Her humor is just a little biting. She keeps Eloise on her toes as much as she provides comfort and support. From what I can tell, they're a spectacular match.

"That's incredibly cool." I lean toward the text. If it is magic, then maybe, just maybe, it can be persuaded to be more useful. "I mean, I can't quite understand the order, but the spacing"—I give a little snap—"it's incredible."

Eloise chuckles softly, shooting me a sly wink as she nods. "You're right there. This book is incredibly neat and tidy. It does a good job of keeping itself presentable." She pats the pages gently. "Let's get to reading. We have twelve pages of Ryans to get through."

I blanch but nod, ready to find out who my parents really were.

CHAPTER 14

ATLAS

"Where has the pest gone to?" I ask Julius as he steps into Darius' office.

"I think she went to visit with Eloise. I believe being a witch is something of a surprise to her." He plops down in one of the chairs we dragged in to make for a more comfortable command room.

"Enough talk of Charlotte." Darius scowls, loosing a sigh before he stands from behind his desk. "Now that we are able to, I believe it best if we begin taking over our old duties," our alpha begins.

Marcus sits across from him, looking dejected but energized. He's been hung up on the pest for one reason or another, and it's making him lose focus. I kick the side of his leg gently and jerk my chin toward our leader as he drones on and on about our old schedules versus the proposed new ones.

I find myself hardly able to listen. He's something like a gnat buzzing lazily at the corner of my consciousness. The extra magic in the castle has been affecting me more since the pest arrived.

Little zaps of it along my skin like playful pinches, whispers of it like a soft song while I shower, and, most annoyingly, pleased little purrs when I go to my room—all causing distractions. I have trouble pulling the magic back once I've begun to wield it, so Darius, as alpha arse, has been keeping it from me.

It isn't my fault the witch is a bad influence.

"Atlas, do you think you're ready for full rotations on your own?" Darius has his arms crossed over his chest, a neutral expression on his face.

I can instantly tell he doesn't think I'm ready.

"I'll join him. It's best not to deviate too much from what worked best before," Julius says before I have the chance to answer.

I bite my cheek to keep the growl in. I want to do this on my own. To show them that after nearly two hundred years of training, I'm able to. They should know by now that they can trust me. As a member of their nest, they should be able to rely on me the same way I can rely on them.

"Whatever," I huff, crossing my arms and kicking my feet up on the edge of our alpha's large desk. My feet slam on the desk, and dirt from my shoes flakes off onto all his oh-so-important paperwork.

"Then that's settled. I'll make up a new schedule, and we'll begin rounds tomorrow," Darius says, shoving my boots off his desk and eyeing the paperwork covered in dark specks.

"Tomorrow!" Marcus leaps up from his chair, wings snapping out and bristling. "We can't, it's too soon, Charlotte is—"

"The witch has nothing to do with this," Darius says with a shake of his head.

Marcus flicks his eyes to Julius and juts his bottom lip out, clearly looking for help. However, the older gargoyle is smart enough not to offer.

"It's already settled, Marcus. There have been some disturbances in Germany again. I need you to go and take a look at those since you know the area. Neutralize the situation as quickly as possible. Julius and Atlas will head out on patrols as well, keeping to Ireland and Scotland. I'll keep my eyes and ears out for anything else, as well as monitoring our sites." He gestures to his laptop like it's the be-all and end-all of everything.

For him, it is. He's the numbers man, the one in charge of everything. What he says goes, no matter how bullshit it is. Julius and I should be going to Germany, and Marcus should be doing the patrols of Ireland, but no. Because I'm a part of the group, we need to stay close to home base where Darius can more easily tamp down my magic.

I scoff, standing quickly and pulling on the leather jacket I had thrown over the back of the seat.

"I'm going out. I want a stiff drink and someone warm against me," I say brashly, not bothering to look at the faces of my nestmates.

Gargoyles are pack creatures, meant to stay together and often meant to share their lover with one another. There is one mate per nest, but with no mate in sight for the hundreds of years we've been together, we're OK with the separate dalliances as long as we make good on our duties.

Marcus makes a soft sound of distress as I pass him on the way out of the overly cramped office.

"Something to say, buttercup?" I ask, pausing in the doorframe.

"You should stay in tonight. Julius is going to make dinner, and we're going to eat with Charlotte." He says it as if there is something to tempt me.

The pest makes me want to rip the castle apart brick by brick, to tear out my insides just to show them to her. It's a volatile feeling I can't stand for more than a few brief minutes.

"No. Anything else?"

"I guess not," Marcus sighs.

"Be careful, Atlas. I want you to go all the way down. No horns, wings, or tail tonight." Darius pulls at the magic shared between all of us, drawing hard on the stuff I'm supposed to be in command of. It gets all twisted up as Darius forces my body to follow his command.

I grip the doorframe harder as a feeling of weakness seeps into my muscles. My smoky complexion quickly turns to that of my human form. The rich tawny color of my skin is pleasant enough, but it never feels like me, especially when I don't make the shift myself.

"Fuck," I hiss, chin dropping toward my chest as I catch my breath. The ache will last the rest of the night. "Did you have to do it like that?"

"It's the only way I know you will actually listen to me."

Colbéliard is incredibly small and feels even more so when I step into one of the three taverns in town and recognize everyone. They surely don't know who I am. The spells we cast keep any of them from remembering us when we venture out.

Striding to the bar, I keep my head down. My normally well-managed hair falls into my face in soft curls and waves. I push it behind my ears, attempting to keep the movement casual. I don't like being this soft all over. It's never felt entirely right.

I take a seat at an empty spot toward the end of the long bar. Sticking to shadows and speaking to as few people as possible helps the magic do its work without disrupting much. But it doesn't stop the feeling of being watched. While they don't outright remember us, mortals often feel like they recognize us, and it's confusing to them when they don't know their brains are repeatedly beaten like scrambled eggs when we want to go out for something as simple as a Guinness.

"What can I get you?" the young bartender asks, sliding over to where I am.

He looks familiar, like someone's kid, but I can't place him.

"Just a pint of Guinness."

"Sure, nothing to eat? We got some fresh meat from the butcher and the—"

"No, kid, fuck off after you give me the pint," I bite out, and his whole body slightly jerks back.

"Got it, a pint and no conversation," he huffs and walks over to the tap, where he begins to fill my glass. "What an arsehole," he whispers under his breath, and I roll my eyes.

After waiting for it to settle, he tops it off and brings me my drink without attempting more conversation, and I pass him my money. I take the first sip when someone decides to take the seat next to mine.

"How are things going?" Eloise asks, leaning away from me, her eyes taking me in from head to toe.

I squirm a little in my seat. This witch is powerful. It explains how she got to be as old as she is, but she makes me uneasy. Almost as uneasy as the pest does.

"We aren't friends. Stop trying to speak to me like one."

She scoffs. "Fine, child, cut your bullshit."

"My bullshit is my best quality," I drawl, taking another sip.

"Charmer, you are. You feel like shit," she says, waving her hand in my direction.

Her magic presses against mine, poking and prodding it, and it sets my teeth on edge.

"Mind your magic," I hiss, not bothering to respond to the blatant callout.

"What happened to you? When you were first brought to town, you were strong. Now you seem much more like a shadow than a valiant protector," she says as she assesses me.

"Nothing happened. My magic is fine, if only limited because of my alpha," I grunt.

"No, there is something else going on." Eloise presses, pushing her magic harder against mine, trying to find a weak point.

"Stop it now before I make you." I bare my teeth.

There's another sharp poke before the prodding stops.

"Is it Charlotte?"

"Why the hell would it be that pest?" I question, lips curling into a sneer.

"She's of unknown magical origin when it comes to bloodline. This might be affecting you more greatly than the others. For as long as I have known you all, you'll never tell them about something that is bothering you unless someone kicks your ass to do so."

"And is this my ass kicking?" I ask with a scoff.

"No, this is the precursor to your ass kicking. Don't make me go to your alpha myself. This situation could be dangerous for all of you if you can't keep your magic under control around her."

"I'm never around her, and I'm going to keep it that way," I say.

Something in the back of my mind tells me I'm going to make a liar of myself.

Eloise gives me a long, hard look, her eyes seeming to glow slightly in the dim bar lighting.

"Sometimes fate has other plans," the old witch says before she pats the bar top and steps away.

She joins a group of older townsfolk with a smile on her face. Their chatter gets lost in the general noise of the bar.

I settle into my seat and sip at my Guinness, enjoying the rich flavor on my tongue.

What does Charlotte taste like?

I jerk in my seat, squashing the thought as quickly as it emerges. I'm here to get away from the pest, to get her off my mind.

"Did you see that hot little feek who moved into the old castle?"

The unfamiliar voice saying those words is like a punch to the side of the head, and my eyes snap to the man who dared to say them. A bloke about twenty stands in a group of other men of similar ages, red faced and grinning. He holds a pint to his chest like it's the only thing keeping him standing, waggling his thick dark eyebrows suggestively.

"The fat one?" another asks, disgust lacing in his tone.

White-hot rage begins to filter in. There are other reasons to put down the pretty pest, the least of which is how she looks. She's annoyingly stunning.

"Sure, she's fat, but she's right pretty in the face," the drunken idiot says, swaying slightly as he takes a step away from the group and toward the old jukebox in the corner.

Everyone knows to stay away from it as it only plays eighties hair metal, The Dubliners, and Sinéad O'Connor. I stand, forgetting my drink on the bar, and intercept him before he gets to the jukebox.

"Not on your life, mate." The growl in my tone is unnecessary but slips out all the same.

The drunken fool looks like he's about to wet himself as he looks up at me. Even being this human in appearance, I'm taller than most and far more muscular than him. His friend that insulted my pest stands, his own cheeks burning from his drinks.

"Let the man play his songs!" he hollers.

I roll my eyes, leaning across the older machine to keep either man from getting to it. My leather jacket squeaks slightly against the dusty glass displaying the CDs and vinyls inside.

"No."

"'Down by the Sally Gardens' would be a good craic right now." The drunkard laughs, his drink sloshing onto his shirt.

"Dubliners? How original." I hold out a hand and gesture back to his table. "Take a seat and stay there, before I make you."

"Outta my way, meathead." He attempts to pull me off the jukebox, and it's all the permission I need to grab him by the scruff and dangle him a foot off the ground.

Sparks of magic ignite under my skin, but I grit my teeth and force it down. Instead, I turn all the built-up ire I've been neglecting onto this unlucky arsehole. I toss him like a rag doll onto his table, sending pints to the floor. Glass shatters and drinks soak the floor. Some of my rage dissipates, but I want to make them bleed for talking about my pest.

The bar is suddenly quiet, the soft sloshing of the wasted alcohol onto the floor the only sound until someone clears their throat behind us. I don't have to turn to know it's Eloise. There's a smugness to the sound that makes me grit my teeth.

"Never speak of her again," I growl, shoving my hands into my pockets to keep from actually spilling any blood.

It would be too easy, and Darius would lose his mind.

I cast my gaze around, unflinching and unapologetic, before storming out of the shitty pub.

MARCUS

When I find my feet carrying me toward Charlotte's room, I don't stop them. I can't fight the urge to be near her. With the mission starting tomorrow, I need to get all the time in with her I can—if she'll take me. I scared her because, of course, I did. I never know when to stop talking, but normally that both gets me into problems and solves them.

How was I supposed to know she had no idea she was a witch? It's strange that some supernatural beings spend most of their lives not knowing what they are, like Char has. My poor witch. The poor, beautiful woman who is my mate.

I press my hand firmly against my chest, trying to stop the hurried beating of my heart. She's going to see us as hers soon enough. I just know it. We're meant to be. The fates decided that long before any of us were even a thought in the universe. Or something like that.

When I stop in front of her door, I shake out my hand before hovering my fist in front of it, the courage to knock slowly draining from me. The last thing I want to do is push her further away. But she's been spending time with the local witches and learning about herself, so she might want to speak with me again. Even if she has been mostly avoiding me...all of us, really. Julius has been making her breakfast and keeping her company, but whenever she sees the rest of us, she bolts to her room and locks the door.

"You can do this," I say with a nod, hand drifting to the door and stopping short as my knuckles meet the wood.

The gentlest knock I've ever made sounds softly in the hall and, hopefully, in her room.

There's no way she heard that, but I did try. I swallow hard and step back, wings restless against my back as I try to keep them tucked, to make myself smaller so she won't be afraid. So she won't run again.

When her door opens, my jaw drops. She's in a towel. So much more of her bare skin is on display than I would dream I'd be seeing this early into the courtship. If I can ever call it that.

When she sees me, she startles, gripping the towel tighter to her body. "Marcus, what are you doing here?"

"In the hallway? Just...walking." I give her a soft smile.

"Just walking in the hall in front of my room because...?" Her words are breathless, her cheeks pink, and her eyes are all over me.

I should feel objectified, but it makes me feel confident. I push out my chest a little and flex the muscles in my arms just the slightest bit.

"Yeah, just patrolling the castle. It's part of the job," I say, leaning back onto the heels of my bare feet.

"Just part of your...protection duty or whatever?" she asks, eyes finally coming up and meeting mine.

My breath lodges in my throat, cementing my airways and leaving nothing but the flavor of her on my tongue. I ache to bring her close. I want to smell the sweat of the day on her skin, bring her to the bathroom, and be the one to wash it all away.

I nod, swallowing thickly.

"Yep, exactly as you said. How has...Eloise been with your teaching?" I ask softly.

She bites her bottom lip, and I hiss softly. I want to pluck the tempting flesh from her teeth and lavish it with attention from my tongue. She's too rough on herself. She's so delicate and soft and should be protected. It's my nest's job to protect our mate, and even with the smallest things, I'm failing.

"It's been OK, confusing and overwhelming if I'm being honest." She slumps against her doorframe.

The towel parts slightly over her plush thigh, revealing even more of her creamy skin for my greedy enjoyment. My knees wobble as the urge to drop to the floor and worship the uncovered inches of skin rises powerfully in my chest.

I've never had a mate before, and inside me, it feels like the most potent magic to exist.

"I bet you're doing an incredible job, though. You seem so smart," I blurt.

She laughs, and her cheeks darken, that shade of pink making me wonder what color her nipples are.

I lick my lips and swallow again, shifting from foot to foot.

"I do my best, but I'm better with a paintbrush than with any sort of books and research."

"Darius could help you. He's the oldest, and he has interacted with more witches than the rest of us combined," I say, trying to be helpful.

Charlotte makes a face at the mention of my alpha but offers a little nod. She rests her head against the doorframe, looking me up and down before blushing even harder.

I grin at her ogling and overtly flex. "It's OK, Char, you can look all you'd like. I feel like I've been working my whole life to perfect my physique just for you," I say honestly.

Her eyes widen, and she digs her teeth harder into that poor bottom lip. I can't stand it.

Swooping in closer, I gently free the abused bit of flesh from her teeth and run the pad of my thumb soothingly over the indentations she made. Her lips part, and I feel her sharply inhale against my fingers as I stroke over her lip.

"You're so soft. I'm obsessed with the way you feel," I whisper, voice dipping low and husky.

A moan slips from between her lips before she wraps them around my finger and gently sucks. Her tongue rolls around the digit, and the magic drains out of me just so I can be softer for her, warmer and more pleasant on her palate. She hums, and it penetrates me straight to the core.

My dick becomes rock hard.

Pun intended.

CHAPTER 15

CHARLOTTE

I MUST BE POSSESSED by the slutty spirit of Kennedy because I've never sucked a man's finger before. Never moaned around the appendage as it shifted from stone to warm flesh in my mouth, and not just because that has never happened before.

I'm more than gone for Marcus. Between his sweetness, earnest nature, and stupidly handsome face, I didn't stand a chance. For him to have genuine feelings for me and not simply return mine feels like a miracle here.

Maybe I used my magic without even thinking about it.

That thought causes me to pull off his finger with a soft *pop*.

He gazes at me with heavily lidded brown eyes. His skin is the color of desert sand, his hair and eyebrows are dark and thick and a little wild, softening up his hard features. He's even more heart-breakingly handsome.

There is *no way* this is real.

"Gods, you're so perfect, Char. Did you know that?" he asks, bringing my fingers to his lip. He gives them a quick kiss before cradling my hand like a wounded bird.

"I don't think so, and you wouldn't either if you were in your right mind."

His head snaps up, eyebrows drawing together in confusion.

"I must have cast a spell on you or something before I knew about my magic. Guys like you never go for fat girls." I grit my teeth against the ache in my heart but power through. I hate spouting this bullshit, but it keeps pouring out. "I'm sorry, and I'll find a way to get Eloise to reverse it. You shouldn't have to be forced to be with me."

"Forced?" he croaks. He looks down at the floorboards, tracing some of the wood grain with movements that remind me of his footwork when playing soccer. "I think—"

A whine fills the air, and I have to drop my towel to cover my ears. The pain of the shrill shriek somehow slips through my fingers and shoots right into my brain. I wince and back up into my room. Fumbling back toward my bed, I crash down onto the soft comforter.

I'll be embarrassed when the pain stops. Marcus will have seen my fat-ass naked, and it'll break the spell, and I'll apologize. He'll be like every other guy, even if he makes me feel unlike any of them ever have.

"Char!" Marcus cries, his pitch nearly matching that of the shriek still ripping through the air. "Are you alright?" he asks, slipping onto the bed.

His weight causes the bed to dip, and I go rolling. My soft flesh collides with his once-again stone body, and I groan but don't move my hands.

"What is that?" I think I ask.

"It's the alarm, the big emergency alarm." Marcus glances back at the still-open door and frowns.

With his face tipped away from me, I think he speaks, but the noise is too loud, and without being able to watch the way his lips move, his words are lost. He stands in a flash, giving me one more sorry look before he rushes out in a blur of yellow.

The second shower does very little to wash away all the self-hatred that has taken root under my skin. Comparison is the killer of joy, and it's never felt more true than now. All the gargoyles are perfect, and I'm conventionally pretty, but not in a traditional way.

I groan and grab my loofah. Scrubbing myself, I give each of my rolls and folds the love they deserve. I take a breath, pushing out the negative voices that live in my head no matter how hard I love myself. It's other people's fault that they don't like me for how I look. I love the way I look and how I feel. Even if I could be carved of stone like them, there's no guarantee Atlas wouldn't hate me, Julius would make a move, or Darius would look at me with more than apprehension.

They'll just have to take me as I am if they want me.

Marcus ran away from me at the drop of a hat when something like a hell siren went off, and I haven't seen him in the few hours since.

"I need more answers," I groan and tip my head back into the hard spray of water, enjoying the sensation of the drops on my skin.

I'm in my head, and I need to not be in my head right now.

"Oh gods, Charlotte, I am so sorry." Darius' voice is the last one I expect to hear when the door suddenly opens.

The tall blue gargoyle stands in a towel at the entrance of the large bathroom, his wings free and tail wrapped neatly around one of his legs.

"Didn't I lock the door?" I ask, trying to cover my body with my arms.

The steam is thick and the glass is pretty fogged, but I don't need two gargoyles to see me naked in one day. Even a witch has her limits.

"It wasn't when I tried the knob." He blanches.

The expression on his face finally shows some of the emotion underneath. There's surprise but not in a bad sort of way. His lips are parted, and his eyes are locked on my silhouette.

Idea.

"Get in and shut the door, please. I need to talk to you about that god-awful alarm," I say softly.

To my surprise, the alpha gargoyle steps farther into the bathroom and whips out his tail to shut the door. The soft snick of the lock sliding into place makes my skin break out in goose bumps.

I'm alone with one of them, and we're both naked.

"Hand me a towel, please." I jut a hand out of the shower while my other hand flounders to turn off the spray of water.

Since the guys have revealed themselves, we've stocked this bathroom with all the necessary soft things, including bath mats and towels.

"Of course." He drifts over to the linen rack and draws out a large, fluffy blue towel. He presses the fabric into my waiting hand as I finally turn off the water.

I pull the towel around myself and step onto the bath mat. Instantly, the difference in temperature makes me shiver, goose bumps becoming even more noticeable on my skin. I shift slightly and tuck my arms around my chest, giving my heavy breasts another layer of protection in addition to adding some extra security to my towel.

"Why did you have me shut the door, Charlotte?" Darius asks, his eyes shining with what can only be the magic inside him. There's no other possible way he could be so luminescent from the inside out.

"That alarm was horrible. It needs to be changed," I say firmly.

"Easily done," he says quickly, the agreement making me feel off balance.

"Oh, well, great," I murmur, my hand drifting to my mouth, and I begin to chew on my nails.

"Is that it?" Darius asks, taking a step closer to me. The towel is warm from the heated rack, but nothing explains the waves of heat rolling off his body as he steps closer, not even magic. "I'll do whatever I can to make you more comfortable."

My breath catches, and I look up into the face of one of the four gargoyles who have made their way under my skin and are closing in on my heart like a deadly infection. My nose wrinkles a bit at the grotesque mental image, but I shake my head.

"I really can't think of anything."

"Not a single thing?" he asks slowly, every word feeling like a separate sentence.

His hands clench and unclench at his sides, and suddenly, warmth pools in my belly.

Fuck, I can only imagine what that movement would look like if he were more flesh than stone, all those delicious veins pressing to the surface of his skin. His perceived strength makes me a little lightheaded, and I sway softly.

"Charlotte." Darius steadies me instantly, the discordant note of terror in his voice like a bucket of cold water dumped over my head. "What's wrong?"

"You and all your gargoyles are making my head hurt. You're too attractive, and I'm way too mortal to deal with this," I snap, clutching the towel tighter around my body.

It's so damn stupid how *small* this gargantuan desire for these monstrous men makes me feel.

He freezes before he laughs in my face. All the carefully fixed neutrality of his expression melts away. His laugh does something funny to my insides, and I can't help but smile right back, a blush that has nothing to do with the steam taking over my entire face. Warmth, joy, and desire quickly overtake any fear that was lodged in my chest. I think I fall for him at that moment.

The light above us flickers, glowing like the midday sun before the bulb hisses and explodes. Glass rains down over the bathroom, and I scream. Darius scoops me up off the floor and tucks his tail over my legs.

He looks up in disbelief. "I didn't do that."

"I think I did," I whisper, blood draining from my face.

Darius' room is attached to his office. I shouldn't be surprised, but I am. I'm surprised he has a room at all—if gargoyles don't actually need to sleep—but he's surprising me more and more with every second we spend in each other's company.

"Alright," he says from where he kneels at my feet, holding one of said feet in his hands as he looks for glass. He strokes his thumb over my arch, and it makes my nipples tighten. "I got you off the floor before you could get cut."

"I did tell you that, multiple times," I grumble, folding my arms over my chest to hide the fact that his touch turns me on.

The sweater Darius gave me is gigantic, and his leather and old book scent wraps around me. I fight the urge to breathe deeply to take it all in.

"I just had to make sure." He lowers my foot toward the floor, but it dangles a few inches above.

His bed frame is high, wrought iron, and thickly made, so of course I can't touch the floor. They're all massive, and even though I'm a few inches above average, they dwarf me.

"I'm so sorry that happened. I texted Eloise, and she said combustion can be a sign that my magic is surfacing more."

Darius glances up at me, reading my expression and smiling. "You're nervous about the magic, aren't you?" he asks as he stands, giving me the best view of his toned thigh and...well, his dick.

The gargoyle is only wearing a tight-fitting pair of boxers that leave very little to the imagination, if anything at all.

I swallow a mouthful of spit before answering. "Who wouldn't be? I didn't grow up using magic or even knowing it was real."

"You're right. You should be nervous. From what I gather,

Eloise thinks you come from a strong bloodline on both sides." He sits beside me casually, his warm thigh pressed against my own.

I'm only wearing his sweater because, of course, I don't have underwear in his room, and he refused to let me go back into mine without looking me over first. He was being such an alpha. It's obnoxious in a way that makes me want to kiss him. It's hard even now to focus on what he said, the whole strong bloodlines thing. And it's not something I want to focus on, so I shift gears, turning fully to face him.

"Thanks for the quick thinking—getting me off the ground— I was about to bolt right through the glass," I admit, cursing the lizard-brain urge to "fight, flight, or fawn."

"I'm a protector. It's what I do," he says, though the way he looks at me makes me think maybe—just maybe—there's something more to his words.

Fuck my brain and those stupid, internalized thoughts of self-hatred that make me doubt and that don't even belong to me. I love fucking and deserve to be fucked, especially by a man who looks at me the way these gargoyles do.

God, I want Darius' hands on me, holding on to me while I blow his mind and he blows mine right back. My eyes land on the growing erection in his boxers, and I gulp audibly.

"I'm sorry, but does your dick have swirls?" I gasp, taking in the details of it as best as I can through the fabric. It's thin but provides enough coverage that I'm questioning what I'm seeing.

I must be daydreaming. I swear the texture reminds me of a certain silicone unicorn horn I've used to get off more than once.

He chuckles and rubs at his jaw, looking away bashfully. "It is. Most gargoyles have a special...texture, if you will."

"Really? Is it the same for everyone in the nest?" I blurt the question out before logic hits my brain.

I basically just asked what the dicks of the other guys I live with look like. I bite my lip and sink down into the plush comforter a little.

Darius chuckles, the sound so delicious it makes my toes curl. "Do you really want to know?"

"I mean, yes, I do, but it's a totally inappropriate question, and I don't have the best track record when trying not to perv on you guys." My cheeks are flaming.

"Well then, I'll give you this hint: we all have differences down there." He gives me a grin that melts the rest of my resolve from my body.

I whimper softly, sinking back against his pillows.

"Wow," I manage.

"I guess so, wow," he repeats, the air around us charged. He leans over me, resting his hand beside my head. "May I kiss you, Charlotte? I can't help but imagine what your lips taste like." The words are a soft confession.

By way of a response, I press my mouth to his and groan.

How do they all feel so dang good? It's not fair. It should be illegal, but I'm going to enjoy it, so send me right to jail.

He deepens the kiss and moves to position himself in a plank style over me. He's too far away, and I don't want that.

I wrap my legs around his waist and pull his body to mine. To my surprise, he comes willingly. He presses his hips to mine, and I feel every glorious inch of his massive cock pressed against my over-heated core. I moan, grinding against him to get some friction. I'm not wearing any panties, so the moment my wet pussy makes contact with the fabric of his boxers, they soak through. I feel the texture of his cock so much better as I writhe and grind my clit against it.

The guttural sound that escapes his mouth as he devours mine is unlike anything a human could make. It's thrilling, a little chilling, and so fucking erotic. His nipples are as hard as the stone they appear to be made of.

"Charlotte," Darius groans against my mouth, nipping and sucking at my top lip gently before giving the same tender treatment to the bottom. "As an immortal, death is never on the table, so your mouth is as close to heaven as I'll get. Thank you." He moves his free hand down to my hips and rocks them harder into his own.

A desperate sound crawls up my throat, and he finally breaks the kiss.

"That was..." I can hardly make out the words as I pant.

I need oxygen, but it doesn't seem like he does.

"Amazing? Perfection? Everything I've been waiting centuries for?"

He asks all those toe-curling questions between soft kisses against my neck. He presses the last one over my pulse, and I know he can feel just how hard my heart is pounding.

"I've never been this wet in my life," I admit, going cherry red.

"Thank you for the honor," he chuckles, bucking his hips gently into mine and drawing a loud moan from my lips. "But I think we should take it slow, leave it to a little extra heavy petting and...not dry humping." He grins at me, and I huff.

"Really? Get a girl all worked up and then leave her hanging?" I complain softly but offer him a small smile to let him know I'm joking...mostly.

"It's important you know about yourself and more about gargoyles before we get into this and it possibly becomes something more," he says, stroking the bare skin of my waist.

I didn't notice him slip his hand under his sweater, but I'm certainly not complaining. I want to curl up and purr like a damn kitten as he strokes me.

"Is there a big difference in dating a supernatural?" I ask, sitting up slightly, dusting light kisses over the bridge of his nose and cheeks.

"With gargoyles especially," he says with a soft sigh. He pulls himself away and stands from the bed. "And with our nest even more so. We have a duty to protect mortal life, and we feel a strong call to do so. We often don't have much time, and things will get worse now that we are able to go out and about as we are," he explains, and my joy begins to deflate like an overused parade float.

"So I'm hardly going to see any of you?" I feel a fissure form in my heart.

"We'll do our best to be around...and, well..." He pauses, biting his lip and taking a long moment. "We're all in this together when it comes to relationships."

That fissure turns into a crack right before my heart splits in two.

"So Atlas will never be on board, and we'll never have a chance."

CHAPTER 16

CHARLOTTE

FOR A WOMAN with four huge gargoyle roommates, I haven't seen or heard from any of them since that day when the horrific alarm went off. The signs of them are still here, the baked goods in the morning and muddy footprints after a hard rainstorm, but for almost two full weeks, I don't so much as see a smudge of color in the corner of my vision. I almost believe this place is just mine again, considering how often they've been away.

I guess that's what I'm telling myself to excuse painting them nonstop. My art room is covered with little portraits of them. Those brief moments of seeing them are etched into my mind so clearly that putting them down on canvas, making them stagnant, feels like a crime.

Tossing aside my latest piece of Marcus' smile, I groan. My hands cramp a little, and I do my best to rub at the joints until they ache just a little less. I can keep going if it's just a little less.

"I have some Tylenol, if you'd like it."

It takes a long moment for it to sink in that I'm actually hearing Marcus' voice rather than imagining it. I turn to face him in the doorway of my studio and jump when I see Julius standing at his side with a forlorn look on his face.

"I'm fine. Always have been and always will be. I don't need protection from my own dang joints," I grumble, turning quickly to keep the canvas I've been working on hidden behind my body. "Why do you have Tylenol anyway? I thought magic would be your cure-all."

"Why did you toss this one?" Julius asks choosing to ignore my question, and I go completely rigid as he picks up the canvas that is much closer to them than it is to me right now. "Oh...well, this is lovely, Charlotte."

A soft chuckle mingles with an excited gasp as the two hold the canvas no bigger than one of their palms between them.

"I knew you liked my mouth, Char. It's missed you nearly as much as I have...My mouth misses yours and you, like all of you really, even if they haven't been introduced just yet," Marcus says with a cheeky grin.

"You are the worst," I groan, pressing my face into my paint-flecked hands.

I can feel the acrylic getting into my fricken pores, but I ignore it and instead focus on the mortification.

"Well, sure, but I also have a pretty mouth," Marcus laughs.

"Any of me in that pile of yours?" Julius asks, and I can feel him at my back.

His presence is so distinct from anything and anyone else. He smells like berries and herbs and citrus from his simmer pots. The ones I find cold on the stove by the time I get down there in the morning to make breakfast.

"This one is incredible," he whispers against the shell of my ear, and I want to melt like a baked candle.

"Which one?" I part my fingers and peek through the space to see him holding one that is part realism and part imagination.

I don't know why I think he knits. Maybe it's because he makes me feel cozy and safe? Or maybe it's because I'm delusional.

"It's really lifelike," Marcus says suddenly, joining the green gargoyle at my back. They're both mostly monstrous and handsome. "Wait a tick, didn't you start that blanket a few weeks back? In the attic!"

I jerk my hands away from my face and turn to them, but since I'm sitting on my stool, my eyes meet the front of their pants. I swallow hard, trying not to imagine what's behind those zippers as I look up and up and up until I reach their faces.

Marcus is the picture of joy and excitement, holding the canvas with his smile in one hand and pointing at the painting of Julius with the other. Julius is cradling the canvas with his visage painted on it and staring with an unreadable expression.

"Marcus, I think you might just be right," Julius whispers, his eyes going slowly from the canvas to me. As his eyes lock with mine, he startles before he smiles. "You did me an incredible justice. I don't think I have that many muscles in my arms anymore."

"Anymore?" I question softly.

"We all used to be way more fit when we were on active protection duty," Marcus says, setting the canvas down gingerly and walking over to the large window that overlooks the area in the front of the castle. The area where he showed me how good he is at football.

"I think you're both still pretty buff, huge actually...like statues," I mumble.

"Like gargoyles," Julius says teasingly, offering me the canvas back. "But we can still gain muscle tone and lose some of it. Magic is funny, especially for those born this way."

"So all of you were born...gargoyles, that is...not made?" I ask, trying to remember the fragments of that conversation. I was under a blanket at the time and quite enjoying how soft it was.

Julius hesitates. "It's a bit of a sensitive subject for some—"

"For Atlas. He means it's sensitive for Atlas." Marcus butts in.

"Right, Atlas is sensitive about born versus made gargoyles

because he was made while the rest of us were born. Other than how one comes to be alive, we are the same at a biological level, but some—"

"Arseholes," Marcus says with a scowl.

"That is the best word for them. They see being made as not as good as being born."

"Well, that explains the chip on his shoulder the size of Texas," I grumble, though I feel bad for him. I've never been so hostile to someone I've hardly interacted with before, but something about Atlas sets me on edge.

"That and the fact that he is the youngest," Marcus says, swaggering back toward me and offering me his hand. "I am the second youngest but the most handsome."

I giggle and slip my fingers into his, spreading the remnants of the paint on my skin across his stone.

"Of course you are," Julius says with a playful roll of his eyes behind the golden frame of his glasses. "Now, shall we do what we planned and actually ask the lady on a date or just whisk her away to it?"

"A date?" I balk.

"A date," Marcus purrs. He pulls me close to his body and wraps his arms around my waist.

"With both of us, if that wasn't clear." Julius pushes his golden glasses up the elegant slope of his nose.

"Darius did say something about you all going for the same girl or something like that." I bite back another giggle of embarrassment.

"When did you talk to Darius about dating us?" Marcus asks adorably, his eyebrows furrowing in confusion.

"There was a little magical incident almost two weeks ago when the alarm went off...before things got all busy," I say, trying not to wince.

"Really? Our alpha?" Julius asks with a laugh. "He's so

reserved, but I'm not surprised you were the one to crack him, darling."

I blush and melt a little on my stool at the tender name.

"I mean, it's a good thing because you're our—"

Julius elbows Marcus in the gut and grins extra wide, sidling closer to me and blocking his nest partner with his wings. "You're everything we could want in a woman. Gorgeous, talented, incredibly sweet, and you like my cooking."

"You're smart too!" Marcus says, grabbing one of Julius' wings and jerking it down to smile at me.

"You two are a lot," I laugh, standing and putting my hands on my hips. "Do I have time to change or...?"

"No need to change. It's a sort of an inside-the-castle date," Marcus says quickly, scampering around Julius and taking one of my hands in both of his. "I don't want to waste any more time. Come on." He begins to tug me toward the door of my workroom before he even finishes the sentence.

Julius follows us with an easy smile on his face.

A room at the top of the tower proves to be the perfect spot for movie marathons. It's the only way to properly use a space where the entire floor is covered in mattresses with enough pillows and blankets to choke a horse.

"This place looks amazing."

"It's our nest!" Marcus beams. "We tend to hang in here when we want quality time. We put in a movie screen, and since there are only little windows"—he points to the small ones toward the top of the rounded room for emphasis—"there's hardly any light to disrupt."

"It's a communal space for us that has a little extra magic to help us recover from any injuries or exhaustion," Julius adds as he settles into a spot against the wall that seems very much like "his spot," with a basket of knitting supplies and a mostly made blanket sticking out. "It's sort of sacred," he says with a smile that doesn't impress the gravity of the space.

Marcus dives into another spot with such force it causes a soccer ball to pop out of a pile of blankets and launch across the room. I squeal and dive out of the way, burying myself in the softness of the floor-bed.

"This is incredible. I swear I've read something just like it in a romance book once or twice."

"Or a dozen times." Julius teases me with a knowing smile.

"Do you read romance?" I ask with a soft, fake gasp.

"Of course I do, it's the best genre." He grins. "I started a book club with Darius about a hundred years ago. It's been the best part of our biweekly forced nest time."

"You're telling me Mr. Serious reads romance too?"

"It's so fucking boring," Marcus groans from somewhere under the sea of blankets.

I push myself up on my elbows, trying to find him. It's hard to lose such a massive man, but in this wonderful mess, I guess it's actually possible. Then I see a blanket move, like something is wriggling underneath, and it's coming closer. As the shape reaches me, I finally see a flash of his yellow tail before Marcus springs from under the blankets and tackles me gently.

"Please tell me we don't have to watch romance movies, pleeeeeease," he begs against the shell of my ear. "I've been eyeing a documentary for ages, and I want to watch it with you, get all of your thoughts on the subject."

I snort and press my face into the blankets, letting a laugh filter out. This feels too good to be true.

"I'm not that smart, Marcus. You're being too kind, but sure, we can watch your documentary," I say.

"Sweet!" he cheers, hopping off me and crawling across the room to a closet built into the wall.

It sits flush with the bricks around it, and I wouldn't have known it was there unless one of them pointed it out. He pops it open and fiddles around with a projector, clicking a button and making a screen roll down to cover the entrance area.

"Alright, let's do this," Marcus says with a bright smile as he lowers the light.

"Are you a cuddler?" Julius asks softly, reaching for me with one hand, the half-finished blanket clutched in the other.

"Very much so," I say, a desperate little trill escaping me as I crawl over and sit beside Julius.

CHAPTER 17

JULIUS

As the credits begin to roll, I glance up, bleary eyed, from my knitting project to see that Marcus has passed out cuddling Charlotte's feet, and she's fallen asleep with her head on my shoulder. The little witch is drooling on my sweater, but I can't muster up the ire I normally would at someone getting my clothes dirty.

I guess this is what it feels like to have a mate.

"You've got to be kidding me." Atlas' voice sounds through the small room before his silhouette appears against the screen. He tosses it up, quickly stepping into the nest with a scowl.

"Kidding you about what?" I ask in a whisper, trying not to disturb the sleeping witch who stirs my heart or the gargoyle who has been my companion for hundreds of years.

The possessiveness that flares to life inside my chest at the look of irritation that Atlas levels on Charlotte surprises me. I'm not an angry guy, much more a lover than a fighter and the poet rather than the soldier, but I want to toss him out the window. I want to drown him in the loch. Even if we don't need to breathe, I want to find a way to make him stop.

I curl an arm around Charlotte's shoulder and stroke at the strap of her overalls. The fabric is well worn and covered in paint, and it doesn't trigger the part of my brain with the impulse to clean. The Gods must be fucking with me, giving me such a messy little mate.

"Oh Gods above and below, Julius, I thought you of all people wouldn't fall for this pest." He clenches a fist and punches the wall without his full force. His magic flares in our shared bond before fizzling down. "She is nothing to us."

"She could be everything to all of us if you'd just give her a chance," I snarl.

Atlas snorts, crossing his arms over his chest and stalking into the room. The blankets suddenly become *dirty*. My mind sticks on the fact, and I growl softly, unable to help the animalistic noise that wrenches from my damn soul.

Our nest is *dirty* because of him and those damn boots.

It's supposed to be a perfect space for us, and we made No Shoes the first rule.

"Stop."

"I'm not doing anything," Atlas snarks before plopping down and making a mess of the arrangement of blankets beside Charlotte.

"You know you're getting on my nerves. You're being a brat," I hiss softly, pulling Charlotte from against me into my lap. I bring my arms around her protectively.

"The pest is too sweet to be savory. Julius. Take your head out of your arse and just look. She shows up the day supernaturals revealed themselves, with the deed to our castle and nary a penny more." He hisses the words with such vitriol it makes my blood boil.

I open my mouth to rebut him, but Charlotte stirs in my arms and yawns softly.

"And you've been nothing but a rude asshole since I showed up. I'm sorry for having the world's worst timing and being poor," she snaps, shifting out of my lap and shoving herself into the small space between me and Atlas.

I bite my lip and try not to think about how her ass is practically in my hand and how fucking soft it is against me and how hot she is when defending herself. Yeah, I see nothing. Nothing going on here. I totally have a hard-on because of knitting. Totally normal.

"What? Did you want me to roll out the red carpet? Well, I'm sorry, I was told at the last fucking minute I'd have to hide in my own damn attic with my nest-mates because there was a confused little pest of a witch coming to town," he snaps back, pushing away from Charlotte.

The beautiful witch scowls and crawls across the blankets to get up close to him again, and though I mourn the loss of her against me, I get an incredible view of her arse in those overalls. I stifle a groan, but Marcus doesn't as he wakes.

"What's with all the noise?" he asks in a sleepy murmur, eyes opening for a second before locking on Charlotte's backside.

"Atlas," I grumble.

"Stop!" Atlas yelps, falling back into a pile of pillows and blankets as Charlotte crawls over his supine body.

I'm jealous of the arsehole because he's where I should be. He's done nothing but be a knob, but he gets straddled...sorta.

"You are invading my personal space," he sputters, freezing up.

"Yeah, well, your attitude has been invading mine. You need to quit it. I'm going to be here until I'm able to get my inheritance and find out more about myself. I didn't know I was a witch when I stepped into this castle, but I'm going to leave knowing everything I need to know about it," she says, leaning down so she's nose to nose with Atlas.

The jealousy burns in my blood, but so does a satisfaction unlike anything I've known. Charlotte is a badass, and she's putting Atlas in his place just like Darius or I would do...though not as gently. She looms over him for another long moment before she pushes herself up onto her knees and then stands.

"I should probably get back downstairs anyway. I want to finish up one of the pieces I was working on so I can start fresh tomorrow," Charlotte murmurs, leaving the nest as soon as the words are out of her mouth.

Marcus's eyes trail after her, and when the door shuts, he sits up and glares at Atlas.

"Really, man?" the happy-go-lucky one out of us asks in a tone very unlike him.

Atlas lies in the blankets with his eyes locked on the ceiling. He isn't breathing, but I'm not entirely concerned. He doesn't need to breathe, and this is just another way for him to be dramatic about everything.

"You need to change all the bedding. I want it washed with the good softener," I growl, shoving to my feet and snatching up my knitting basket. "Every single piece, Atlas."

"Yeah, you know shoes are a no-no in the nest," Marcus says, providing unnecessary but helpful backup.

Atlas has yet to speak and continues to stare straight up at the rafters.

I storm from the nest and head toward my bedroom. The door to the armory is open a crack as I pass, but I don't linger. The last thing I need right now is to accidentally snap at her because Atlas got me all riled up.

Stomping into my room, I slam the door and slide the lock into place. The room is a mess, unlike the way I like to keep the rest of the house. This space is a piece of the deepest recesses of my mind, so in here, things can be wherever the hell I want them. I toss the basket down beside the door and pick up the blanket I had been working on the day Charlotte arrived. It makes me think back to the conversation with Marcus and how he chose a blanket over a scarf. Maybe it was supposed to be for her.

ATLAS

I swore I would never share breath with a witch again, yet there I was, with a witch in my face, practically tasting the magic rolling off her skin.

I press my lips together after a moment and hold my breath.

The sensation of her hovering over me makes my entire body tingle, like a million fire ants biting into my flesh all at once. I may be stone, but even I have had the occasional flesh-side accident, and she feels like that but a million times worse.

Gods she is so much fucking worse than anything I could have ever imagined and so fucking perfect it makes me ache. She left me here on the floor, just staring at the ceiling. Marcus is still here in the nest that I've sullied, glaring at me. I can feel the air of his judgment and do my best to focus on that instead. It hurts to be near her, but it's agony to be any distance away.

Finally, I release a breath, and Marcus snorts.

"We don't need to breathe. That's not very impressive." He scoots over to sit beside me.

Too many words are swirling around in my mind to string the perfect ones together into a sentence to tell him to fuck off. So I don't. The ceiling is the only thing that makes sense at the moment. It's high above me, the ancient wood beams still sturdy and strong from our years of care. They won't change on me. The ceiling beams will stay the same as they have for hundreds of years.

"I can tell you like her," Marcus says, and my entire chest constricts.

A wheeze of air rushes from my deflated lungs, and he laughs.

"You think you can hide behind all that brooding, but we're nest-mates, man. I can see through you in a way no one else can," he adds with a far too chipper demeanor. "You like Charlotte, and it scares the shit out of you because you haven't had the best experiences with witches, especially strange ones."

"You don't know anything about my experience with witches." The words come out in a defensive hiss, more reflex than intention.

"I do so." Marcus scoffs. "I know you were made by a witch who abandoned you, and ever since, you haven't trusted a single witch we haven't vetted with about a hundred years of time first." He then flops down beside me, looking at the same beams that make up the ceiling.

"I don't have to trust witches," I grumble, finally letting my eyes shut.

The pain of the memories Marcus just pulled to the surface rushes to the forefront of my mind. If only it had just been abandonment.

"The pest has gotten you all twisted in knots, Marcus. We can't trust her."

"And why not?" he asks with a petulant little cluck of his tongue. "She's sweet, sexy as hell, and she's been painting us nonstop."

"That doesn't make her case any better." I furrow my brows as I imagine it. Paintings of all of us in her little art room, my old armory, and something like elation rolls through me. I bite hard at my cheek, not letting the emotion show on my face.

"You should ask her to see them, Atlas. They're incredible. She did this one of my smile, and I just like...Well, I didn't think my smile was anything special beforehand, but seeing myself through her eyes—" His words are cut off by a dreamy sigh that makes my whole body heave up off the floor.

"I'll think about it after the sun has exploded," I huff. Yanking up the blankets I'd been lounging on, I move around the room and pick up every bit of linen I can fit into my arms.

"Or you could stop being so moody and just get to know her.

She said she wasn't leaving, and both Julius and I plan to court her. I think Darius might be planning to as well," Marcus says as he folds his arms behind his head and smiles widely.

"You've got to be fucking kidding me," I groan.

"Nope."

"She's got Darius thinking with his dick now too?" The question is harsh, but everything about that witch makes me want to start thinking with my dick too.

She is incredibly thick all over and so fucking soft. Her body hovering over mine was a test of my willpower to the highest degree. I wouldn't do a thing without her consent, but I have a feeling she would have given in if she'd felt my hard body pressed tighter to hers.

A soft, shuddering breath escapes me as Marcus stands and gathers the rest of the blankets I can't carry.

"I'll help you bring these down to the basement." He flicks his eyes around the room in one final check for any missing linens.

"Thanks."

"What are nest-mates for if not for helping you with shit you don't wanna do." He laughs and bounds out the door and down the stairs. "Last one to the laundry room is a rotten egg!"

I roll my eyes but instantly have a better idea. I press myself to the wall and close my eyes, willing the castle to let me through, and in that same breath, I can taste the boggy air. I clutch the bundle of sheets and blankets tighter as I dive off the tower and plunge toward the ground, catching myself at the last minute with my wings. I land with a thump and sprint for the door. I kick it open and speed toward the basement, where the kitchen, cold storage, and laundry areas are. I come to a halt at the bottom of the stairs.

Julius has his arms around Charlotte, their mouths slotted together with not a breath of space between them.

I can practically see her tongue fucking into his mouth from here. My wings flex and smack against the wall, but I'm too distracted to care. She's kissing him like there's nothing she would rather gulp down than his fucking spit.

Envy flares inside my blood, but I stomp off to the laundry room before they pull away and catch sight of me.

Marcus arrives a few minutes later, panting to seem more mortal as he drops the blankets.

"How did you get down here so fast?" he asks with a frown.

"I'll never let you know my secrets." I snicker, gathering up all the things that need washing and tossing them into our two separate washers.

The drums are huge and give the items enough space to slosh around and actually get clean. The machines are a recent addition to the castle. Julius much preferred when our laundry was done by hand, so we know how much time and effort it takes to get blood out of fabric. But modern technology was just too good to pass up.

Marcus taps his fingers along the buttons just to make them light up, and I scoff. "Really?"

"Duh, you need to, uh." He pauses, then looks at what he just clicked. "Need the extra wash cycle and extra soap."

"Extra of the magic soap that should clean every linen thing in this castle with just a few drops? Obviously, we need more," I say with a roll of my eyes.

"It smells good!" Marcus argues with a whine that nearly makes me miss the slight squeak of the door creaking open.

My eyes slip from my nest-mate to the inquisitive set of eyes peering in at us, and I stiffen, arms folding over my chest in an instant.

"Don't just stand there and gawk, pest. Come in if you must," I snap.

The door slams open, knocking against an antique washing basin Julius keeps around for shits and giggles before she stomps in.

"So you're washing everything, like Julius asked?" Her tone is confused, part question and part defensive posturing.

She seems as confused as I feel.

"The nest should always be kept tidy," I intone, remembering all the lessons Julius taught me when I first arrived.

Back then, the castle and surrounding town were so different. It's hard to consider the two the same place, even as I've watched the centuries go by.

"Good," she sniffs, looking at the huge washers and dryers lining the wall of the cramped room. "He should have made you do it by hand. He was telling me you were always the person to come home with the most foul clothing after missions."

The barest hint of a smile curls at the edge of her lips, and I want so badly to run my tongue along the seam of those post-kiss pink lips.

I clear my throat and shrug. "I'm a little messy, so what?"

"A little?" Marcus snickers. "You basically had half of the loch on you. A few years ago, all you had to do was deal with the kelpies, and you made it seem like you saved the world!"

A few years ago was actually about fifty years ago, if I remember the exact incident correctly. The kelpie didn't exactly like that I was wearing clothing in the first place, so they dragged me through the mud for nearly half an hour until we hit a rock, and I used it to get myself free of their hold. It was one of the most annoying things I've had to deal with when it comes to any sort of protection work, supernatural or mortal. Kelpies are dickheads.

"It's good you're taking responsibility." Charlotte steps farther into the small room, and I retreat on instinct to avoid her touching me again.

A very thin sliver of faux annoyance and posturing keeps me from just grabbing her and kissing the daylights out of her.

It wouldn't *not* make her a witch, but it would make her shut up for a moment, and I think that might improve my liking of her. She makes me burn all over, but clearly she's doing something far more to my nest-mates. I want to experience it too, if just for a moment, what it would be like to be entwined with her instead of melted into a puddle of stupidity and anger in the wake of her mere presence.

"Hey, Char, do you wanna come to my room and see all my balls?" Marcus asks, sensing the tension growing thicker in the air and doing his best to cut it.

The witch giggles and takes the hand Marcus offers. He sweeps her out of the room, and I crumple against the wall, breathing hard.

Why is she so stupidly perfect?

CHAPTER 18

DARIUS

I'm used to spending long days and nights alone in my office. Now that Charlotte has arrived and has slowly been growing closer to me and my nest-mates, I find it hard to sit here and focus when I could be with them.

Pushing away from my desk, I pop my back and groan, allowing myself to run through the magic that binds the nest together. Nothing feels out of the ordinary.

Our magic has been strange since Charlotte arrived, and I was beginning to believe what Marcus had said.

Mate.

Soulmate.

Fated mate.

All words with the same meaning—this witch is the center of our nest.

Blowing out a breath, I groan again. "Atlas will never let that happen."

As if summoned by the mention of his name, Atlas bursts into my office with his wings flared in agitation. He grunts as he knocks down nearly a dozen books from my shelves.

"What is it now?" I ask, even though I don't want to get into this.

"The witch. You can't be seriously falling for the games she's playing," he growls.

Something's off about him. The magic within the bond snaps and writhes between us. I could pull back, know that I should, but I also have a desire to see this through at least a little.

"She is a very nice woman, Atlas. You should give her a chance," I say through gritted teeth, knowing none of the words I say will get through to him.

His trauma with witches makes it understandable that he wants nothing to do with them, but this is fate, and fighting fate will get us nowhere.

"I refuse. I refuse, Darius...You cannot make me tolerate her." He barks the words out. All snarls that suddenly become clear.

He's afraid. Putting on some kind of act to hide how he feels.

A soft rumble of understanding vibrates in my chest. "I'm not going to make you. I may be your alpha, but I am no taskmaster. Though it would be harsh to call falling for a beautiful witch a hardship." I snicker.

Atlas grunts and begins to pick up my books, some of that rage simmering down, as if he forgot to feel it in the moment.

"I want solo assignments, Darius. I can't be around you all when you're falling at her damn feet." He stands and reshelves the old tomes, some older than he is. "Marcus and Julius brought her into the nest, and that is where my line is."

"They brought her into the nest without us?" I ask, the shock like someone dumping cold water over my head.

"I see they haven't gotten around to telling you yet. They are far too busy shoving their tongues down her throat," Atlas says with a roll of his eyes.

"Well, I'll have to speak with them both, then. The nest is

space for us to go and feel safe. You know that as well as I do, and they should know it as well." I think back to the time many years ago when the only place Atlas could find peace was in the nest, surrounded by us as we lent him our strength to fight the demons waging inside him.

There are things he never told us about the witch who created him—the foul man who still haunts his darkest dreams on nights when we all feel helpless—but I know he never had anyone care for him before. As a member of my nest, I will always care for him and try to put his and the rest of our nest-mates' feelings above any others.

That doesn't include Charlotte. Yet.

The thought of forsaking her is like a shot to the gut.

"As for the solo mission, we will discuss it, Atlas. You still have much to learn about drawing your magic back. You're good with letting it out, but wielding it is a different story."

"I can wield my magic just fine. If you let me have more of it from time to time, I would be able to practice," he snipes.

"Earn it. It may be yours, but I am the keeper of all our safety, and giving you more magic would be like handing you a loaded gun with a fifty-fifty chance of a backfire."

"Fuck you," Atlas snaps.

"Fuck you right back." I shrug and stride over to him, pulling the younger gargoyle into my chest and giving him a tight hug.

"You are mine to protect as much as the mortals are, Atlas. Keep your head, and we will figure this out. Charlotte is not like your maker," I whisper softly, trying to keep my voice even and clear of the heavy emotions that threaten to break me.

Atlas shudders in my hold before he pulls free without returning my hug.

"This is fucking ridiculous," he growls and storms out of my office with the same force he came in with.

I should go talk to him, but at the same time, a bigger discussion needs to happen with Julius and Marcus. As the alpha, I'm juggling everything, and now is not the time to let a single ball fall.

I dig into my pocket, pulling out the old copper coin, rubbed smooth on both sides from centuries of contemplation. I flip the smooth disk and let it land against my palm. I close a fist around it and stride from the office with much more tact than Atlas.

CHAPTER 19

CHARLOTTE

TALK ABOUT SOME *BALLS*. Gargoyles are weird. They can be any color of the rainbow, and their dicks are wild. I know because I'm currently staring at one that makes my mouth water.

Marcus gulps audibly and flexes his abs, his cock bouncing with the move. It's beautiful and sunshiny yellow like the rest of him, but it has ridges. Every quarter of an inch or so, and there are a lot of inches. From this position on my knees, he feels even more huge, both in cock length and stature.

"You're looking at my dick like it's going to bite you. I promise it hasn't bitten me yet, and I give him some rough treatment." Marcus jokes with a waggle of his brows.

He's full-on gargoyle right now, with the wings and the tail and the inhuman hotness that makes my ovaries weep. My tongue darts out to wet my lips as I ogle him.

"I don't think it's gonna bite me, but I think I have a one-hundred-percent chance of choking," I mumble, shifting to sit my ass back on my heels.

All this feels like an incredible escalation from our date. One little snuggle in the most amazing nest, and suddenly, I want to bang all their brains out, even Atlas. It's horrible how wet I get just thinking of him glaring at me. Their attention is the most potent aphrodisiac known to *me*.

"We don't have to do this if you're uncomfortable." Marcus' eyes widen, and the concern that shines in them makes me want to shove his whole cock in my mouth, choking be damned.

"I'm not regretting this, just a little...surprised to encounter my first supernatural cock."

"First and one of your last." He winks. "My nest and I are going to fuck you so good that you never want to leave us."

I snort at the thought of Atlas putting his dick anywhere near me, and then I'm thinking about it. His dick. Atlas' dick is probably fucking glorious and as bratty as he is.

"This feels really weird, but really right," I admit, getting back up on my knees and leaning over his massive thighs.

They're so fucking strong and hard underneath my soft skin. It makes me ache to feel his rigid length in my throat.

"I know exactly how you feel, Char. No one has made my body sing like you," he says softly, bringing his hand down to cup my cheek.

I press my face into his palm. If I were a kitten, I would be purring up a damn storm.

Marcus makes me feel so fucking safe and beautiful beyond words.

I need his dick in my mouth. Right. Now.

A shiver of anticipation works its way down my spine. I've never been so turned on by the idea of sucking someone's dick, but Marcus, my sweet gargoyle, is not like anyone else in the world.

He grabs the base and holds his cock to my lips, and the feel of his dick is unusual and pleasant. He's hard and warm but not as hard as someone made of stone should be. He has a give to him that tells my hindbrain this will very much work.

Slipping the head past my lips, I groan at his flavor, rich and musky with a sweetness that makes me want to take him all the way to the hilt. I'd need a jaw like a snake to do it, but if there's something worth dislocating your jaw over, I'm pretty sure it's this. Hollowing my cheeks, I sink down an inch, one of his ridges popping into the tight ring of my lips. The sensation makes my teeth vibrate a bit, but his groan is so worth it.

MARCUS

My sexy as fuck witch has my dick in her mouth.

My eyes are currently in the back of my skull, trying to find any logical thought left but coming up with nothing.

I don't need thought when I have her plush lips wrapped around my hot, hard cock.

I groan like a fucking beast as she hollows her cheeks and gives me a hard suck.

A burst of pre-cum floods from me and hits her hot tongue. I try not to pull back, but she's going to make me come *waaaay* too quickly if I don't.

Easing a hand into her hair, I gently guide her mouth off my cock, which she releases with a satisfying pop.

"I was just getting to the good part. I do this little thing with my tongue." She pauses and presumably does it between her closed lips.

I've never wanted to get my dick back in a hole so quickly.

"I don't want to come too quickly." If I were in my more mortal form, I would be blushing so hard my ears would be bright red.

Charlotte arches a brow. "Can't hold back, even a little?"

Her tone is all challenge, and Mama didn't raise no quitter. Mama actually hardly raised me.

Oh well.

"Try me, babe," I say, taking a quick breath and then holding it. Which really does nothing.

Charlotte leans down and takes my cock back into her mouth. I groan behind clenched teeth and try to focus on the patterns in the wallpaper. The wall sconces are nice and shiny in here. I wonder if Charlotte polishes them, or if the resident gargoyle mom that is Julius sneaks in here to make sure her entire room is nice and tidy.

The head of my cock hits the back of Charlotte's throat. And then she swallows.

An unholy bellow pulls itself from my chest, and I grip her shoulders as gently as I possibly can.

"Fuck, yes, that's a good girl, Char. Fuck me, your mouth is heaven and hell all in one," I moan.

She does the thing with her tongue, twisting around each of my ridges as more of my hard length press into the tight, warm embrace of her mouth and throat. She giggles around my cock, and it's like someone took a pleasure Taser to my balls. I keen, back arching and toes curling.

"Jesus, Mary, Joseph, and some other guy, fuck!" I cry as Charlotte blows my mind with her mouth.

Her hands rest delicately on my thighs as she bobs her head and sucks my soul out. I flop back onto the bed, only able to lie there and take every bit of pleasure she gives me.

I wish I could be inside her forever.

CHAPTER 20

CHARLOTTE

Marcus somehow tastes like cake. I don't know what part of my mind either shut down or woke up, but his cock in my mouth is heavenly, and from the way he groans and grabs my hair, it is for him too. I'm drooling like a fiend and trying to slurp it all back in as I bob on his length.

The ridges prove to be a nonissue as I curl my lips over my teeth to protect both them and him. His pre-cum is so salty and sweet I want to put it on ice cream. I grip his thighs as tightly as I can, pleading without words for him not to move an inch as I gorge myself on him.

"Charlotte." Marcus moans my name like an agonized prayer.

I grant him no mercy as I lash my tongue over the head of his cock, lapping at the weeping tip. I feel like a woman possessed, and it's actually really hot.

I slide my hands from his thighs to my body, which has slowly grown hotter with each suck on this handsome gargoyle's cock. I squeeze my breasts through the thin cotton sleep shirt I picked out, thankful for it being pretty threadbare so I can feel the warmth of my hands. I groan around Marcus as I pinch and pull at my nipples. The little buds tighten to stiff peaks.

"Fuck me, you are so beautiful, so fucking hot. I want to lick every inch of you," the gargoyle pants, writhing in pleasure.

I've never felt so powerful. With my mouth on this man's cock, he would do anything I asked. Hell, I think he'd do it even if his cock wasn't in my mouth. But still. Marcus is just about the sweetest man I have ever met, even if he dropped the fact of me being a witch on my head like a sack of bricks, and I think I'm ready to fuck him.

Oh my fucking gods, I want to fuck him.

I pull my mouth off his cock, panting softly. The realization feels a shit ton more significant than any of the sexual acts I've done.

"I want to have sex with you," I blurt, my cheeks heating.

Marcus' head lolls to the side, and he looks down at me with a smile. His cock bobs, and I swallow. "I was hoping you'd come to that realization. I've wanted you to fuck me since, like...the second day we met, almost the first day, but I didn't want to be too weird."

I snicker and press a kiss to his thigh as I stand, pulling off my sleep shirt and tossing it into the corner. My whole body is bare to him now, and I do my best not to suck in. Even if I feel like the baddest bitch there is right now. It's hard to keep myself from overthinking about how my belly jiggles as I climb onto the bed.

Straddling his thighs, I slowly crawl up his long body until the ridge of his cock presses against my sex. My pussy is weeping all over him, and his cock jerks, happy to be showered in my lust.

"We don't have to do this if you aren't ready," he says in a dazed voice as he slips his hand from behind his head to rest on my hips.

"I know. I want this so badly." I gasp softly as I lift my hips and his cockhead notches at my entrance. He's fucking huge, and it's not even in yet. I'm going to die on his dick, and it's going to be epic. "Jesus."

"Nope, just Marcus," he says as a joke, gently stroking my skin with his thumbs until I finally get the courage to sink down just a little.

His cock head finally breaches my tight pussy, and I mewl like a kitten. The stretch is fucking divine, the little sting hardly noticeable in comparison to the tingles of pleasure that race through me. With another panting breath, I drop myself down onto the rest of his cock.

We cry out together, and I think I can see heaven. The clouds part, and the shiny pearly gates have a No Entry sign posted.

"Oh, Charlotte," Marcus hisses, sliding his knees toward my back until his feet are flat on the bed.

He bucks up inside me, and if he weren't already pressed tightly to my cervix, he would be battering it into oblivion.

"Marcus," I moan, scrambling for purchase on his stone chest.

I finally grab his shoulder, leaning over so my breasts are in his face. My spine is a little stretched, but it works, and the discomfort is more than worth it when he takes one of my aching nipples into his mouth and sucks.

I whimper when he expertly rolls his tongue around the aching bud as he fucks into me from below. The pleasure is never ending, and all too soon, the pressure of an orgasm builds. I groan and dig my nails into his stone skin. The slight give telling me he's alive is the only thing keeping my nails from cracking.

"I'm going to come." I whimper again, head tipping back.

He releases my nipple for a moment. "Then come and keep fucking coming. I'm not stopping until we've ruined this bed."

The growl of his words vibrates against my overly sensitive skin before he goes back to work on my breasts, switching from one to the other at a maddeningly quick pace.

The sharp zaps of pleasure from my nipples and the staccato pounding in the deepest parts of my pussy, his ridges massaging my walls and stroking over my G-spot with every thrust—combine all that with the stretch, and just fucking do me in.

With all those ridges, I never stood a chance.

I shatter around his cock with a cry. My orgasm makes me shake and quiver on top of him, my hips rolling and rocking to drain every ounce of pleasure from this.

He groans like he's in torment but keeps up the pace, never once slowing down or letting his hips stutter.

"Coming...again," I croak, the pleasure not letting me get a proper lungful of air.

I don't fucking care, though, because this orgasm is even better than the first. It leaves my vision fucking white, and my toes curl as I squirt all over the gargoyle fucking me into oblivion.

"Fuck, yes, Charlotte, I'm going to come in this tight little pussy," he groans, letting his head tip back against the bed.

He tightens his hands on my hips and picks up his speed, pounding into me like I'm nothing but a doll for his pleasure. It's something I never thought I would be into, but it gets me the hell off.

I whine from the intense pleasure as my pussy doesn't stop spasming around his length. Then, an intense flood of heat fills me as Marcus groans. His cum fills me up and spills out, coating the insides of my thighs and going all over him.

He flexes his fingers against my hips before he slips his hands up my spine and brings me down to lie on his chest. The tender touches make my cheeks heat, my chest filling with adoration. He's warm and solid beneath all my softness. The contrast between us is beautiful and feels so dang good.

Shivering lightly and panting, I press my face into his rock-hard chest and giggle. "That was incredible."

CHAPTER 21

CHARLOTTE

FOR THE NEXT THREE DAYS, I'm basically jelly. Julius brings me breakfast in my art room and sits beside me for hours, reading his book while I paint. I think I'm finally getting over my incredible obsession with each and every detail of these handsome men as I begin to paint something abstract. A bunch of colors that collide in ways that make something inside me stir.

Eloise thinks my magic likes to express itself through my paintings, and I'm starting to believe her.

"Char! You have got to see this." Marcus comes tearing into my art room, holding up a small black ball.

"What's that?" I ask, thinking of all the sports I know and coming up very short with what that might be used for.

"Fuck's sake, Marcus, put that thing away. I don't think Charlotte is ready for that," Julius laughs.

"It's sort of like...well, it's basically a courting gift, but like, will you be my girlfriend sort of thing." Marcus stumbles over his words, and his wings tuck against his back shyly.

"You want me to be your girlfriend?" I ask, startled.

I drop my brush into a water cup and stand, rubbing the smears of paint on my palms onto my overalls.

"Yes, and I'd like to fuck you with Julius, right here right now." Marcus shares a look with the other gargoyle, his tentative smile turning into a confident grin.

My jaw drops.

Julius laughs again, but he gives me a heated expression from behind the golden frames of his glasses. He wants me too. I know he does. He's proven as much with his actions if not with his words.

"Marcus and I were having a little naked chat in my bedroom when he mentioned how perfect you'd be between us," the green gargoyle says with an easy smile.

"You want to fuck me in my art studio?" I ask slowly, looking around for a space clear enough for any of us to be laid out on. My eyes snap back to them. "You two fuck?"

"We have for many years," he says offhandedly. "I take it you like the idea of being between us, then?" Julius rises from his seat and places the book on the stool. He strides over and sits me back down, pulling me and my hot seat toward the center of the room. "You have to accept his gift first, then we'll fuck your brains out."

Marcus nods and offers the orb to me. Closer up, it looks to be made of marble or some other kind of deeply dark rock that can also have a million different colors in it. It's beautiful and reminds me of all four gargoyles, even if only two of them are presenting it to me.

"Yes, I will be your girlfriend." Joy fills me and overflows like a million champagne bubbles.

I didn't know either of these men a few months ago, but I was willing to jump right into this with them. It feels right and better than any relationship I've ever had.

JULIUS

Darius is going to kill us, but I can't seem to find it in me to care as Charlotte takes the nest's heart into her palms, gazing at it with reverence. Marcus and I are being more than a little bit sneaky doing this, but she is worth it.

To say that the heart is a courting gift is like calling a cannon a "little gun." There is nothing more significant in the courting rituals of gargoyles than giving your mate the heart of your nest, and somehow, Marcus stole it out of Darius' office without him noticing.

"Should I put this in my room first?" Charlotte asks, finally looking back up at us. Her eyes are a little glassy.

"No, I've got a box," Marcus says, pulling out the small, dark wooden box the heart has been kept in since our nest was first formed.

He carefully takes the heart and sets it inside the box. When he clicks the little latch closed, Charlotte jolts a bit.

"He's not taking it away, just putting it somewhere safe. I want to make you go wild, little witch," I purr against her ear soothingly as I kneel beside her.

It's so strange to have such a little mate. Gargoyles normally pair with their own kind or with creatures who can physically withstand lovemaking with gargoyles in full monster form. I'm afraid I'm going to break the little witch.

"You're all talk," she says, locking eyes with me suddenly. She licks her lips and leans in, kissing me hard.

I return her kiss with the same fervor. I'm not all talk, and I'm going to prove it to her. I've wanted to touch every inch of her body since she first stumbled into my kitchen while I was making a protective simmer pot. She stole a hot muffin, and I was petrified she had hurt herself, but holding her then and having her skin against mine was the best I'd ever felt.

"Such a good witch, isn't she?" Marcus asks from beside us.

"I'm not good—" Charlotte pulls back from the kiss, choking on her breath as she tips her face to see Marcus has already stripped naked.

His clothes lie in a haphazard pile in front of the door, like that would do anything to keep the other two out of the room if they really wanted in.

"You are so good, the best." Marcus joins me on his knees at the feet of our witch. "You took my cock like a champ baby. You have to show Julius how well you take it."

I chuckle and nudge him aside.

"It's my turn to stuff our witch full, bastard. You can lick her clean."

Charlotte blushes, and Marcus groans at the mental image.

"Can I?" he asks Charlotte. "Can I clean your pussy out with my tongue after he fills you up? Please, Char?"

She nods, looking back at me. "You, um...like that sort of thing?"

"I like anything when it involves you, though I would prefer we keep body fluids that aren't spit, cum, and other natural lubes to ourselves," I murmur, weaving one hand into her hair.

I grip at the base of her skull and tip her head to the side. The pretty pale column of her throat is exposed to me, and I attack it with my lips and teeth. I leave little trailing bruises until I reach her shirt.

"She is wearing way too many clothes," Marcus says and unclips her overalls, tugging them down. He lifts her with one hand and pulls them over her hips.

Charlotte squeaks and grips his shoulders. "Easy," she yelps, not used to being manhandled.

"You're right. It is easy to lift you, easy to put you in any position we want, easy to fuck you as long as we want," I growl.

The desire to do just that is almost overwhelming me.

"Please, just fuck me before I completely ruin these panties," she grumbles, and Marcus finally exposes them as her overalls come off.

Her panties are so fucking soaked, her sweet scent making my mouth water.

"Such a dirty little witch. You need us so badly," I croon, jerking the crotch to the side to get a look at her glistening pussy.

My cock punches against the zipper of my slacks, aching to get inside our mate, but I need to take things slowly. Even if she has taken Marcus' cock, I'm the longest out of us all, and it'll be a challenge to get every inch in.

"Fuck," she moans as I lean in and lick her from entrance to clit, swirling around the sensitive bundle of nerves as I plunge a finger in. "Right there."

"Demanding, isn't she?" Marcus asks with a chuckle as he pulls her shirt up and off over her head.

I can only catch the barest glimpses of the rest of her body with my head between her legs, but I wouldn't want to be anywhere else.

I devour her pussy as I stretch her with my fingers, keeping my attention on that spot that makes her cry out and moan. Her sounds are so damn good. I can't get enough of them, but when her thighs begin to tremble, I pull back.

"You are to come on my dick, not my tongue or my fingers," I rumble before diving right back in.

I lash at her clit with my tongue and curl my fingers against her G-spot.

"Not fair!" Charlotte cries, her body spasming.

Marcus has moved behind her and is holding her body to his hard chest. He has her arms behind her back, his lips beside her ear, undoubtedly whispering filthy things about "nothing being fair."

I groan as I'm rewarded with a gush of her pleasure. I yank my fingers from her pussy, and she keens, pouring onto the floor. I toss my sweater off, then push my pants down enough to free my cock before adjusting myself and thrusting halfway into her with a single movement.

Her tight pink pussy stretching around my emerald-green shaft is like a work of art. I'm already glistening with her arousal, and her warm, velvety walls are milking along my rigid shaft. I have to grit my teeth to keep from embarrassing myself like some youngling. One hand drifts down, my thumb strumming her clit.

"Fucking hell!" she whines, her hips bucking. Her eyes fly open, and then she shoots her gaze down to where we're connected.

"Holy shit, too long, abort mission," Charlotte pants, looking up at me with startled eyes. "It's not going to fit. It's not gonna happen. I have organs!"

"It's going to fit. Your body was made to fit our cocks," I purr, running a hand through her hair. "I'll take it nice and slow so you can get used to the feeling of being stretched around me. Just relax, and if it hurts, tell me."

"Fuck, go slowly, please." She whispers softly and I lean down to press a soft kiss to her lips.

"I never want to hurt you, just breathe."

She nods, panting as she tries to relax against Marcus. Her breasts heave in my face, and I bury my face between the two soft mounds.

"Fuck yes," I moan, the softness of her skin so damn incredible.

I edge my hips forward a little more, working my cock inside her a half inch at a time. Her pussy drips around me and swallows me down with little flutters of pleasure. As much as her mind doesn't think she can take me, her body sure as hells wants to.

CHAPTER 22

DARIUS

I've only ever thought about killing my nest-mates once. Today marks the second occurrence of such bloody, violent thoughts.

How could they?

Which one of them did it?

I fight against the anger to keep it from clouding my judgment. I am the alpha of my nest, and I will bring them to heel. Clearly one of those arseholes took the heart to give it to Charlotte, so either Marcus or Julius—who am I kidding. Marcus took it.

"Golden retriever bastard." I seethe, pushing away from my desk, kicking one of the drawers I yanked from it in my haste to find the item that was the thing keeping our nest together.

He doesn't know what the heart of the nest really means, not gifting it or even showing it to another person. He could be royally screwing us without even knowing it. I doubt Charlotte would even know what to do with the heart, but still. As a witch, she has the power to take from it, destroy it if it pleases her. The thought makes me flinch, and I grip the doorframe of my office. Staring into the hall, I try to think of where Marcus might be with it and if I can get it back before Charlotte knows of its existence.

Not five steps down the hall, I hear it. Cries of ecstasy.

"I'm too late," I growl, taking off at a run to chase down the sound.

Standing in front of our old armory, I pause, the sounds of mingled pleasure overwhelming me. I am just as enraptured with Charlotte, and that could be me in the room with them, gifting her something that would mean she is ours forever. But no. Of course, Marcus had to sneak around behind my back and ruin this. He's too kind for his own good.

I pound my fist against the door, and I hear Charlotte shriek.

"Go away!" Marcus calls from somewhere deep in the room.

"Stop what you are doing at once. If you want to cover yourselves, I'm coming in."

I should have just burst in. There is no need to be kind at this moment. I've seen both Marcus and Julius naked, and I want nothing more than to see Charlotte naked. I've felt her body against me, but to see her in all her glory would be an entirely different thing.

I bite my knuckle to keep the groan that rattles my chest from slipping out.

I know this witch is our mate. I feel it in the threads of my magic, but still. Trust needs to be earned, and when gifting the heart, all members of a nest need to trust the one receiving it. Atlas can never find out, or he's going to have a heart attack.

"Come in," Charlotte squeaks.

I shove the door open, kicking aside Marcus' clothes and taking in the trio. Julius and Marcus are standing beside Charlotte, regarding her with intense eyes. Julius' clothes are rumpled, and his jumper is hanging from a windowsill rather than on his person. Marcus proudly stands buck naked to one side of the witch, who has pulled a paint-splattered apron over her body.

She blushes furiously and can't seem to meet my eyes.

The box containing the nest's heart sits precariously on the edge of a stool, and I hiss at the sight of it.

"You are a fucking fool," I snap at Marcus, storming over and snatching up the box.

Charlotte jolts from her stool and lunges for me. Her tiny hand grips the opposite side of the box, and I swear.

"What are you doing?"

"I don't know," she whispers, blinking up at me, but her hand doesn't move from the box.

"We all know it's hers. Just give it to her," Julius says, one of his hands drifting up to adjust his glasses, but they aren't on his face, so it falls to his side uselessly.

"That is not how this works." I'm trying to contain the agony roiling inside me.

"Marcus gave it to me. Doesn't that make it mine?" Charlotte's voice is trembling as she asks me the question.

Tears pool in her eyes, and I swear again, letting her take the box.

She scrambles back to the other two gargoyles in the room and holds the box to her chest. "I'm...I'm sorry, I don't know what came over me, but this is mine," she says firmly.

I want to puff with pride but can't seem to find the energy to feel the necessary emotion. I huff, running a hand through my hair. Between my office and here, I must have softened myself down, gone mortal in a sense to appear less threatening.

"I know it is. I don't want to take it from you," I tell her gently. "But Atlas...he doesn't seem keen on courting you, even if we all are. It's not fair to him."

"What isn't fair to me?" Atlas asks, striding into the room with a casual disinterest that shatters the moment he sees the heart's box in Charlotte's hands.

CHAPTER 23

ATLAS

No.

> *No.*
> *No.*
> *I do not belong to a witch.*
> *I will not be owned.*
> *Not again.*

CHAPTER 24

CHARLOTTE

ATLAS FREEZES, staring directly at the box in my hands. I clutch the special rock closer and turn slightly away.

"How could you let this happen?" Atlas lashes out at Darius, picking up an empty canvas and tossing it at the other gargoyle, who switches from his more human appearance to his supernatural form in the blink of an eye.

Darius goes to catch the frame, and his claws shred the canvas. He grips the canvas and growls at the younger gargoyle. "Go to my office."

"Fuck your office," Atlas barks, a laugh of pure hysterics ripping from him. "Fuck you all. How could you allow this pest to come between us?"

"She isn't a pest," Marcus snarls, snaking his arm around my waist and pulling me to his still-nude body.

"You know as well as we all do that she is our mate, Atlas. Even if you haven't allowed yourself to recognize it." Julius gives a sigh of frustration. "I am sick of this, hiding that we want her."

"Mate?" I croak. "Like in those werewolf romance books?"

"For fuck's sake," Atlas hisses, spinning toward the door, whipping his tail and wings out in anger. "Of course you know what those supernaturals need, but gargoyles? Noooo, not us. We aren't *important to witches*."

I'm struck by the rage and hurt in his voice, the venom with which he calls me a *witch*. I pull myself closer to Marcus and Julius, trying to weather the emotional whiplash as it rolls through me. Both gargoyles holding me stroke my spine, trying to soothe me without being overt about it. Tears fill my eyes, and I clutch the box with the orb thing to my chest. I want to keep it so badly, but if Atlas is this hurt, then maybe I should just let it go.

"What the fuck? I'm doing my best here!" I snap, voice thick with emotion.

Something in my core ignites—the magic inside me, I guess. My fingers pleasantly tingle where they touch the wood of the box, an acknowledgment of my already-formed connection.

"Atlas, you are being too harsh on her." Darius suddenly loses his steam as he finds himself between his nest-mates.

The pale blue gargoyle's jaw tenses and flexes, again and again, as he grinds his teeth. He can't even tell which side is the right one now.

"I'm sorry it hurts you, but this belongs to me now," I say, trying to sound confident. My hands tremble as I hold the box so tightly my knuckles go white, and my fingers won't loosen, even when I try to force them.

"I'm done, with all of you." Atlas' voice is devoid of emotion, and his cool gray eyes go from looking at me to piercing right through.

He walks out of the art room, and I can hear his footsteps get farther and farther away.

"What the hell just happened?" I ask in a whisper, looking between the three remaining gargoyles who are frozen. "What the fuck just happened?" The pitch of my voice rises, and goose bumps break out all over my skin.

I flex my fingers and finally pull them free of the box as I set it in my lap. The weight of its importance fills me with excitement and dread that sinks into my stomach like lead.

"You look pale. Sit down by the fire, and I'll make some tea," Dara says as soon as she sees me standing on their doorstep.

I didn't know where else to go. After Atlas stormed out, the rest of them dispersed, first to their own rooms and then to the four winds. Probably to search for the broodiest and most insufferable gargoyle of the lot.

"Thanks," I mutter numbly as I step inside and take a seat by the fireplace.

Eloise comes into the living room with a yawn. She's wearing a flannel over a soft gray pajama set, and I'm jealous of the flicker of adoration in her eyes as she spots her wife. They hold each other's gaze for a moment, having a silent conversation that all partners seem to be able to have after they've grown to love one another with their entire being.

I dip my head so I don't have to watch the moment.

"Charlotte, it's good to see you. How have your exercises been going?" Eloise asks as she takes a seat on the couch.

"Fine, I'm not any better or worse." The words feel heavy on my tongue, but I force them out.

"Here you are," Dara says softly, offering me a cup that I never saw her go to the kitchen to retrieve, but I take it anyway and swallow a mouthful of steaming liquid.

"One of those days," Eloise sighs.

"You could say that."

"Do you want to tell us about it?" Dara asks as she sits beside her wife, concern carving deep lines into her delicate features.

Eloise takes one of her wife's hands and holds it on her lap.

"I think I broke them," I whisper, not wanting to share the shame of what I caused with anyone.

I'm out of my depth, and there is no way I could go to Kennedy for advice like this.

"What do you mean?" Dara asks at the same time that Eloise says, "You need to speak up. We're not that young anymore."

"I broke them!" I snarl suddenly, the fragile thread of numbness snapping.

My body begins to shiver, and the dark tea in my mug ripples and pops, magic leaking from me like an old faucet.

"How did you break them? Gargoyles are damn near immortal beings. I'm sure they're alright if it was just a chip," Eloise says with a little laugh, though her expression tightens when she eyes my cup.

"It's not funny! None of this is funny. All I've done is ruin their damn lives by coming here. They don't deserve a mate like me," I sob.

The sea of emotions in my chest quickly churns from anger and strife to sadness so all-consuming I want to let it drag me under. I set the roiling tea down on a small table and press the heels of my hands into my eyes to stop the tears from flowing.

"Atlas, he took off. They haven't been able to find him. They looked for hours," I croak, voice cracking with emotion.

The tea hisses and spits like a cajoling crowd.

"How long has he been gone?" Eloise asks, leaning forward and releasing Dara's hand. She waves a finger over the tea, and it settles in the mug.

Dara stands, muttering something to herself and sweeping out of the room.

"I think it's been almost twenty-four hours now. I haven't been able to sleep." I wheeze, pressing my face harder into my hands. "I'm so fucking worried."

"So one of them spilled the beans about being your mate and

he took off. Atlas is sensitive with witches. You have to understand." Eloise reaches over and pats my knee gently.

"He thinks I hate him!" I sob, finally unable to hold it back any
longer. I lift my face, the hot tears and snot running like rivers
down my face.

"Don't you? The last time we spoke, it didn't seem like you
liked him very much at all." Eloise shrugs lightly, her eyes watching
my every movement intensely, like I'm going to snap and set her
house on fire.

Who knows? Maybe I could actually do it with my magic, if
only it did anything when I called to it.

Eloise stares with wide eyes at me as I whimper and sniffle, hot
tears rolling down my cheeks.

"What am I going to do?" I croak, wiping my face on my sleeve
for lack of something better.

"Do you want something stronger than tea?" she finally asks.

I laugh a little, the sound broken and small. "Yes, please."

Eloise stands and goes over to a small cabinet. She bends down
and begins looking through bottles. The soft clinking of glass and
release of emotions finally begins to calm me a little. I lean back
into the chair and shut my eyes, trying to keep my breath steady.

Atlas will be fine. He's a strong, hard-headed jackass, but he
isn't stupid, and he's old. Not as old as the others, but he's built to
be a defender. Built, not born like the rest of them.

Therein lies the problem with me and him. A witch did
horrible things to him that I will never understand, but all that
hatred falls onto me; all witches must burn and suffer his anger
because of one horrible asshole from his past. I wish I could find
who made Atlas and rip them apart with my bare hands, or unleash
the magic that roils inside me on them. The thought alone makes it
swell in my soul, like a storm you can sense due to the shift in ozone.

"Here." Eloise presses a cool glass into my left hand, and I
blink my eyes open.

The glass is filled nearly to the brim with a dark amber liquid. I bring it to my nose and instantly regret it as a strong alcoholic scent kicks me in the teeth.

I wince, and Eloise grins.

"That will more than make you feel better," she says, returning to her seat on the couch.

"Thanks." I raise the glass a bit before bringing it to my lips, shutting my eyes and taking a deep drink. I swallow and swallow even as it burns. All the way down, I can feel the liquor scorching until it reaches my stomach.

I cough when I finally stop guzzling the hard liquor. Half the glass is empty. "Better already."

"Sure you are." Eloise gives me a tight smile, and Dara finally comes back into the room.

In her arms are the strangest things I have ever seen. Plushies. Four different plushies—one yellow, one green, one blue, and one black. Gargoyles. They're gargoyles, and they're all dressed like the gargoyles they are modeled after. *My gargoyles.*

"Why the hell do you have those?" I give a startled squawk.

"Part of my magic is connected to the soul and, in turn, soul-mates. It's not an exact science because magic never is, but I had a feeling I would need to make these soon," she says, coming over and setting them in my lap.

I involuntarily melt into the seat, whatever magic in them comforting me bone deep.

They're about twelve inches tall and surprisingly heavy for their sizes. I lift up the Marcus plushie and nearly drop it when I feel his familiar warmth.

"These are magic stuffed toys. They are connected to your mates. You'll be able to feel their heartbeats and their warmth," Dara explains, her cheeks darkening slightly.

"She did it so you'd know that Atlas is alive. If the asshole goes cold or you can't feel the heartbeat, then at least you know," Eloise says, crossing her arms over her chest.

I gape at the plushies in my lap, sitting them up and looking into their adorable button eyes.

"They're so cute." I can't help but gush over them, gently running a fingertip over the small details.

Each of their horns is different, like they are on the real-life version, and their expressions capture their personalities so well. Atlas is even wearing a little leather jacket and smirking like the jerk face he is.

"Thank you so much."

"Of course." Dara gives me a bright smile. "They are yours to keep. I can only ever make them once, but they should be as indestructible as your men."

I pull them to my chest and give them the biggest squeeze. "I'll take care of them, I promise."

Just like I'll take care of the real ones, if they let me.

CHAPTER 25

JULIUS

My simmer pot boils over, causing the flame under it to hiss and pop at me. I blink down into the water, unmoving, as cranberries, orange peels, and little bits of sage float to the surface.

I'm doing this because I do it every day, but it doesn't feel right. Nothing has felt right since Atlas left. The young gargoyle may have been loud, annoying, a bit of a mess, and afraid of witches, but he was my nest-mate, a friend and companion.

I let him down. I didn't help him prepare for what life was going to be like.

How could I have? I didn't know Charlotte was coming to us. No one knew it was going to happen. She just appeared like a strike of lightning and left us all irrevocably changed in her wake.

"Good morning," the witch says suddenly behind me.

I wasn't paying any attention, or I would have heard her like I did on that first day.

"Good morning. Did you get any sleep?" I ask, turning to look at her.

It's hard to be a functional mortal being with everything she has been going through. I'm glad for the first time in my life that I only need an hour of sleep to be completely functional and rested. I wouldn't survive otherwise.

"I did, actually." She gives me a small smile.

Her hair is sticking up slightly from where she slept on it, and her face has soft lines from her sheets and pillow.

I want to cup her face and smooth the lines away, kissing her until she is well and truly awake, but touching her feels like a betrayal so deep I can't stomach it.

I give her a tight smile and point to the fridge. "I made some yogurt yesterday evening, and there is some fresh fruit with it."

"No baking?" she asks, eyes scanning the counters for my usual mess of fresh baked goods.

Empty.

"No, I couldn't really focus," I admit, stirring the simmer pot and swirling all the ingredients into a whirlpool.

You aren't really supposed to impart any discord into the magic, but it's all I can seem to feel, so it seeps in, just a touch.

"Oh, OK. How have you been sleeping?" she asks, walking over to the fridge and pulling it open. She pokes around inside before pulling out a package of strawberries and the yogurt. "Have you been sleeping?"

"As much as I need," I reply, trying to skirt around the fact that I would be exhausted otherwise.

"Hmmm." She sits down at the island, grabbing a large bright red berry.

She pulls the cover from the yogurt container and dunks the fruit right in. I wince at the cross contamination, the move reminding me of something Atlas would do.

She takes a bite of the fruit and moans. "This is so good. How did you make the yogurt?"

Her curiosity is almost enough to dull the ache in my chest.

"Instant Pot and a little bit of either already-made yogurt or

175

cultures you can get from the shops," I reply, stirring and stirring the pot.

"It's really, really good. Thank you for making it."

"Of course, I need to keep the nest well fed." The words are weak, barely a whisper.

"Oh...Julius." Charlotte stands up and rushes to me, crushing me from behind in a tight hug.

"I'm sorry. This is all my fault."

I feel her tears seep into the fabric of my sweater and grip the wooden spoon tighter.

"It's not your fault. It's all our fault. We were too gentle with Atlas. He should have been going to therapy." My shoulders slump. "We failed him long before you came along."

"I didn't help at all, and yeah, I think we all need therapy."

I sniffle, and I can feel her wipe her nose on me.

I grin just a little and turn around in her arms. I pull her closer and rest my chin gently on the top of her head.

"He'll calm down and come back. He has to."

CHAPTER 26

CHARLOTTE

ATLAS IS NEVER FAR from my mind. Three days into his tantrum, I'm more than sick of being alone. I miss all my gargoyles, but the guilt eats away at me like acid. He didn't want me because of his deep-seated hatred for witches, and we should have been able to work that out together, but I got too excited by the possibility of orgies with four hot supernatural dudes to think clearly.

I've never been this physically interested in anyone before, and suddenly, creatures I would, in theory, run screaming from are just drawing me in deeper and deeper.

Burrowing into the pile of blankets I've amassed, I slide a hand out from under the pile and pull the plushies into the space one by one. Laying them all beside me, I sigh and curl the Atlas one into my arms. I can feel a steady heartbeat, strong and defiant against my chest.

"I know we haven't gotten off on the right foot," I murmur softly against the plushie's gently pointed gray ear. "But we all miss you. Your nest-mates most of all, of course, but I do too. I haven't gotten to know you at all, and I'm already halfway in love with you."

Of course, the stuffed Atlas doesn't respond, but I swear I can feel the heartbeat picking up against my own. I hold him tighter, hugging the absolute crap out of this tiny magic version of my soulmate.

The steadiness of his heartbeat and warmth radiating off all my tiny mates settles me right to sleep.

DARIUS

Out of everyone, I should have known better. The oldest is supposed to be the wisest, but clearly I never got that memo. The formation of this nest had been a fight from the very beginning. Atlas never knew what to make of his place in our nest, and now he's gone, and I finally have to confront the fact that I've failed him. Julius and Marcus are good friends. But me? I've always gotten along better when I have someone I can take under my wing both physically and metaphorically.

Atlas was the one who relied on me to know what to do in a split second, and I let him down when it came to the expanse of our future. I was lax with our other nest-mates. Julius and Marcus took our affections for Charlotte too far, way too fast for Atlas to handle. I'm supposed to be able to mediate my nest, but I've failed royally.

Giving a mate a nest's heart is deeper than marriage, and Atlas knew that better than the others. He always believed he had something to prove, so he became our encyclopedia. When we all came together, it was Atlas who began crafting the heart of our nest and made sure it was absolutely perfect for our future mate, whoever they may be. It was never a question of if he was good enough, but he made it seem that way. The chip on his shoulder from being made always made him feel inferior to us, even if we didn't see it that way. To us, he was always just one of us.

Sadness makes my stomach burn, so I do the only thing I can think of and pour myself another two fingers of scotch. I take the short glass and swirl the dark liquid, drinking it in one pungent mouthful before setting the glass back down on the small chair beside my favorite seat in the more formal sitting room.

The fire crackles in my periphery, and I wonder if I can pay Eloise or Dara enough to track Atlas down for us. He hasn't been spotted by any of our nearby allies, so the worry keeps mounting in my chest.

There seems to be no way to get to him until he chooses it, and it frustrates me to no end. He hasn't even reached for the pool of magic that we share, or I would be able to follow that pull like a trail of breadcrumbs.

"Where in the world are you, youngling?" I muse aloud, tipping my head back and shutting my eyes.

"Please, don't make me go back." The youngling's voice cracks as they tremble so hard I'm afraid they may crack a wing.

The tree they picked may be large, but the cavity they are hiding in is narrow and more than too small for them. This tree is on the edge of the forest, closer to the small village nearby, and well used by the local children. When some of them had come screaming about a monster, I knew I had to investigate. The rains that are common in this part of the world pour down as I land. I had ignored it, but it must have covered him from my notice on patrol.

I slowly lift my hand and extend it toward him with my palm up.

"You don't have to go back. You don't have to go anywhere you

don't want to be," I say coolly, my face impassive and unmoved by the situation that is actually tearing my heart from its place in my chest.

"I never wanted to be made," the youngling sobs.

The tears rolling down their cheeks are an acrid green, the chemicals and magic that give them their life not yet settled enough not to seep out.

"I know, none of us ask for life, but we must take it." I gently set my hand on their forearm and draw them from the shadowed nook of the great oak tree. "And we must use it for good."

Their skin is dark, gray and black speckled. They're a handsome youngling with long black hair still damp from being caught in the rain before finding shelter in this tree...and taking down one of its largest branches in the process.

"I do not know—" Their breathing is hard, the sharp planes of their face etched with fear. "I do not know how to do anything like that. Goodness is a concept unfamiliar to me."

"Good can be taught. I find that the goodness you gather is more worthwhile than anything instilled in you," I croon and draw the youngling farther out.

They are large but still a foot shorter than me. Their eyes flick around quickly, trying to perceive a danger that is nowhere around. The short horns on their head end in sharp points, and they tip their head toward the slightest creak and groan of nature as if they mean to gore whatever comes at us.

"What is your name? Do you prefer something different—" than what your maker gave you? The question dies on my tongue as the youngling looks at me with wide eyes.

"No, no name to call my own," they murmur.

"That won't do," I say softly, with a shake of my head.

The youngling winces and curls in on themselves.

"But that isn't your fault. We can find your name together. Would you like to come and meet my friends?"

"Friends? Witches?" they ask in a distressed hiss.

"No, gargoyles, just like us." I slowly tug them toward me, and they come, still trembling.

"Gargoyles, meet more gargoyles," they murmur with a quick jerk of their head. I assume it's affirmative. "I can do that."

"Still haven't picked a name?" Marcus asks, leaning over the chessboard that Julius and I are using to get closer to the gray youngling who has been studying our moves with careful eyes.

The youngling's eyes shoot up and across to the gargoyle who is most unlike themselves in our nest.

"Not yet," he admits, rubbing the back of his neck.

He may not have chosen a name, but he has told us that he is a male like the rest of us and seeks a partner of the fairer sex, the same as we do.

"What about Onyx?" Marcus asks with a wide grin. "You're not quite the right colors, but it's cool, and your eyes are pretty close."

The youngling shakes his head. "No, not quite right," he says with a sigh. "But I can feel it. I'm close to figuring it out."

"Take your time. Gods know, I wish I could have gone by a different name," Julius says, though he doesn't entirely mean it.

Julius did change his name when he joined us and dropped the one that belonged to his family.

"I have narrowed it down." He gives a slight tip of his head. His hair is shorter now, almost to his shoulders and wavy.

He is a pretty one now that his features have settled and he is nourished.

"Care to share?" I ask, making a move that I know was unwise.

The corner of the youngling's mouth kicks up as he winces. "Did you mean to do that?" he asks in a barely concealed whisper.

Julius laughs, putting me into checkmate. "Darius likes to let me win from time to time. It keeps up the morale."

Marcus chuckles before joining Julius in a laugh that makes me flush with embarrassment. My eyes flick to the youngling as a smile captures his lips, and then he, too, is laughing at me.

"Atlas, it's go time!" Marcus whoops as he leaps over the thick wooden railing of the grand front stairs.

He lands with a thump in the entryway, and I give him a withering look.

"Careful, this castle is ours now, and we need to take care of it."

A shadow whizzes into the room, nearly knocking me over. The magic it brings into the room stalls my lungs, but I smile. Sparks of green, blue, and yellow fly off him as Atlas makes his stop beside Marcus. He's grinning, no longer the uncomfortable youngling he was a few decades ago.

"Think you can keep up with me, old man?" Atlas snickers at Marcus, who gapes at him.

"I am not old! Darius is old!"

"Enough of this, both of you," I say with a chuckle. "We have patrols to begin."

A sudden knock thunders into the small space. Each of us stands at the ready as I stride toward the door and pull it open, appearing like a mortal. The man in the door is of middle age, with some graying at his temples and an air of displeasure so thick it could choke me.

"You have something of mine, and I would like it back." His voice is gravelly from disuse, and I catch sight of his yellowing teeth.

He reeks of death.

"I have never seen you in my life. Who might you be?" I ask, trying to keep my temper.

My instincts instantly dislike this man, and the pinch in my gut tells me something is terribly wrong.

"Do not play coy with me, boy. Give it back to me, or I will make you regret it," the old man snarls.

His teeth, now more exposed, show further signs of decay, a sign of prolonged use of the darkest magic.

My eyes widen, and I stumble a step back before someone is at my back, catching me.

"You have no power over any of us, and you have no power to make demands of the Colbéliard nest." Atlas' voice is sharp and cold, slicing like an obsidian knife.

The old witch's eyes widen, and he grinds those vile teeth together. Magic, the same acid green I remember from that night beside the tree, rolls off him like mist from the loch.

"You worthless whelp, cost me more to put together than you were ever worth. If you will not be of use to me, then you deserve to return to dust."

Atlas stiffens, and I stand more squarely in front of the younger gargoyle.

Putting myself between him and his maker, I tell the witch, "Atlas is one of us."

CHARLOTTE

I startle awake sometime later, tossing the blankets off from over my head. The room is pitch black around me, the night having settled in while I was dozing.

Fear and adrenaline that don't belong to me course through my veins as I come down from that dream. *Anger. Disgust. Pure terror.* The frightened youngling's emotions—*Atlas'* emotions.

"Those were not my dreams." I scrub my hands over my face, trying to ignore the urge to rub that stink off my skin. "Gods, that guy smelled terrible."

Atlas' maker was one ugly son of a witch, who certainly was not kind or good. Of course, he doesn't like witches and seems to merely tolerate Eloise when she visits. Even if I didn't know I was a witch, he knew from the moment I stepped into their home and took it over before basically demanding that things go back to normal for them.

My own world might have been flipped by supernaturals, but Atlas' world had been shoved into a blender and set to high by me.

Atlas was the one who really needed me the most. He pushed and pushed because he thought I would be the same as his abuser. I did nothing to reassure him I was different. Reaching for my plushies, I pull Darius, Marcus, and then Julius into my lap before taking Atlas and holding him to my chest. His heart beats but not as strongly as before, his warmth fading against my fingertips.

"Oh no."

CHAPTER 27

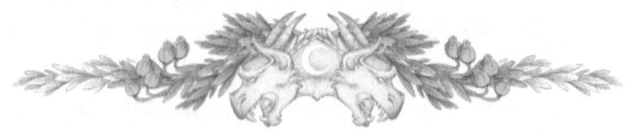

MARCUS

SITTING at the top of the castle always calms me down. Darius is going mad with worry, and Julius has gotten all sullen. I can't even help Charlotte feel any better, no matter how much I try to make her laugh. The only place I'm any use to them is on the roof, playing lookout.

Atlas has been gone for two weeks, and we've searched everywhere. Well, everywhere in Continental Europe and the Isles. But that is everywhere. Crossing into other protected territory would only cause more problems. Atlas was good at sticking to our places and coming back, but apparently, this was just too much.

It's my fault he's gone. I'm the reason everyone is so upset.

The thought of just letting myself drop from this astronomical height flashes across my mind for a moment before I shake it away. That wouldn't help anyone, and I know we'll figure this all out. We have to figure this all out. Charlotte is meant to be ours, and Atlas will see that...one day. When he comes back.

Swinging my legs, I stare into the distance, watching heavy dark clouds roll in. Finally, the rain will come in and clear all the heavy feelings away. With a dejected sigh, I lie back on the roof and shut my eyes.

The splash of the first cool drop on my skin makes me shiver and smile. It's followed quickly by a thousand more, drop after cool drop. The thoughts racing in my head slow down as I focus on the feeling as each drop hits my skin and rolls. Fuck, it's almost as good as eating Charlotte's pussy. The calm that settles over me is something I haven't been able to feel since Atlas left.

I lie in the rain for a long time before the thunder and lightning start. Behind my eyelids, the flashes of lightning are even more beautiful as they make the world a little brighter surrounding our loch. The heavy rumble of the thunder leaves me feeling alright enough to let my mind go utterly blank.

I'm pretty sure this is meditation or something. I should tell Darius to try it out, maybe it will help him with all his stress.

I almost don't hear it. The scream that tears through the night between cracks of thunder, but I know that voice. I know who's screaming.

My eyes shoot open, heart thundering as the beating of wings fills the air.

"Marcus!" Atlas' voice is pained, his scream shattering at the end.

He has his arm gripped tightly around his chest, something thin and gold spewing out from where his arms meet.

My mouth drops open and doesn't close again until he's closer and I can see that something is very much not right. Atlas is flying strangely, his body not looking quite right. His face is twisted in agony as he flies closer, a large golden streak running across his dark chest.

I brace to hop off the roof and help him when he flies over as quickly as a shot, the golden liquid running over his skin, dripping like the rain and splattering against my face.

Warm, thick, and tingling with magic. *Blood*.

"Atlas, what the fuck happened?" I ask as I scramble to follow him.

He can't seem to stay in the air now that he's in the vicinity of the castle. He begins to tip to one side and then the other. He swings like a pendulum, and it makes me choke on my panic.

I bite on the inside of my bottom lip to keep the sound in as I take to the air and fly after him.

Atlas groans, the sound soft and weak, as his wings begin to slow. He loses altitude fast and comes crashing down in our front yard.

I zip through the air after him and land on my feet beside his body. My magic pulses inside me. I can feel every inch of my body from the steady thrum of power I'm trying to pull. Darius jerks it right back through the bond, and I huff, falling to my knees.

"Hey, buddy, what happened?" I ask, trying to take stock of the massive injury.

Atlas rolls over to look up at me, leaving a small pool of golden blood where he was once face down. His expression pinches tighter, and he tsks through gritted teeth at me.

"Well, I went for a fucking walk—" He starts to sass, and I just *snap*.

"Fuck off!" My voice cracks with the thunder, and Atlas' eyes soften.

He coughs and groans, some of his golden blood dribbling from the corner of his mouth.

My heart stalls in my chest.

"Please, just tell me how to help you." My hands are shaking as I lift them over him.

I'm not a healer by any means, but our magic is linked, and I should be able to do something for my nest-mate.

"Can somebody help us?!" I call in the direction of the castle.

"There is nothing to do," Atlas whispers.

When I look back at him, a dusty tone colors his skin, which can only be from the blood loss.

"You're being crazy. We're immortal," I say with a forced laugh that splinters and cracks on my tongue. "You'll be fine, I just know it, and then you can kick Charlotte out or whatever you want." I ramble as my eyes find the cause of all that bleeding.

From his left shoulder all the way down to his right hip, his body isn't fucking connected. Gold weeps from the huge wound in his side, and I feel puke creep up the back of my throat.

I didn't know gargoyles could puke, but Atlas's injury lances me straight through with terror.

"Please come quick!" My voice snaps through the air again, but I can't take my eyes off Atlas.

He doesn't look too good, and if I take my eyes off him, then he might not be there when I put them back.

I rest a hand gently into the tangled waves of his hair, not knowing what the fuck to do. I'm a protector, but here, I'm utterly helpless. I can't do anything to save my nest-mate, and I just might blow it worse this time than ever before.

"You would really let me kick out our mate?" Atlas asks suddenly, his eyes unfocused and pointed toward the dreary sky.

"Yes, but you have to live. This nest is nothing without you, Atlas." I give his cheek a gentle pat, trying to keep him awake. "You need to keep your eyes open, or I might vomit on you."

Atlas takes in a deep breath and winces. "Don't do that, don't make me want to laugh."

"I'm sorry, it's a gift." I frown and bite my cheek. "You just have to stay awake. Just keep your eyes on my handsome face."

Atlas snorts, some of that cool, give-no-shits-take-no-shits attitude showing itself.

"Handsome face, my ass."

CHAPTER 28

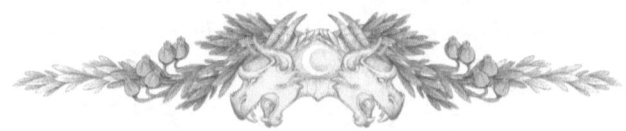

JULIUS

Selfishly, I'm watching Charlotte work in her studio. Something about the way she works and moves and expresses how she feels without knowing I'm there makes me feel less horrible for avoiding her.

We've all been avoiding her, and I think she's avoiding us right back. It's only fair, but you don't have to like what's fair.

Charlotte has always made me feel a little selfish. I love it when she eats the breakfast I make for her, knowing I'm the one giving her nutrition to have the energy she needs to get through the day and to sustain the magic that flows through her veins.

Lurking in the shadows of the doorway to her studio, I feel much more like a demon than a gargoyle. My magic allows me mastery of the castle in a lot of ways. Molding the shadows to my body is tricky but manageable. I greedily drink in her body as she moves from the window to her easel, painting the thick dark clouds with streaks of golden lightning.

She captures the color so vividly. If I didn't know any better, I would think she is painting with gold rather than acrylics.

The rain patters down on the roof high above us as I watch her paint. Each little flick of her wrist adds another smudge of color, adding to the painting that seems to be just as alive as the force of nature it's capturing.

Lightning strikes close, and she flinches softly as the quiet in the studio is broken. Rain taps against the large windows, making the warm light of the room dance slightly. Her breath catches for a moment, and I feel the experimental prod of her magic. I have to bite my lip to keep from moaning. It's not an inherently sexual touch, but I'm starved for Charlotte.

"How long have you been standing there?" she asks, setting down her palette and brush.

She shoves her hands into the front pockets over her overalls as she turns to face me.

I release a soft breath and let the shadows fall from my form. "Not too long. I can't help myself knowing you're right...there." I lift my hand and reach for her before jerking it back.

"I am right here. I didn't go anywhere, Atlas did," she snaps, eyes misting over, her pretty pink lips twisting into a mixture of a grimace and a frown.

I flinch at the harshness of her words, pushing my glasses up the bridge of my nose to give myself a fraction of a second to think.

"He did, and he was wrong for expressing his hurt like that, but he will be back, and we'll work this all out. I can feel it." I press my free hand to my gut. "It's worse than indigestion."

My attempt to lighten the mood falls flat as her gaze withers.

"You're so lucky you're cute."

"Just cute?" I ask softly, my booted foot toeing the line between the hallway and her studio.

I want to take her into my arms more than anything.

"Really fishing for a compliment, aren't you?" The smile on her lips tells me she doesn't mind my teasing.

"Well, the best compliments come from pretty witches—"

"Can somebody help us?!"

190

"Please come quick!"

Marcus' sharp calls for help send a bolt of panic straight through me. I swear if he fell off the castle again trying to practice his landings, I'm going to kill him myself.

Charlotte's eyes go wide, and I can see as magic makes the ends of her hair whip up. The air tingles with it as it seeps out of her, but I can hardly tell the difference between her power and my mounting anxiety.

"Stay here," I yelp as I rush out of her studio, pulling on the nest's magic to speed up my steps inhumanly.

It takes me two panting breaths to go from the warmth of the castle out into the rain. Then I see why Marcus is screaming.

Atlas.

CHARLOTTE

Trust your gut.

Eloise's words ring clear in my mind the moment after Julius zips from my studio. More of a green smudge than a gargoyle.

There was something in Marcus' voice that has never been there before. Even from this distance, I could practically hear his fear, and it makes my heart race.

I take off after Julius, trying not to trip over my feet as I scramble down the stairs of the main entryway and through the still-open front door into the yard. Julius, Darius, and Marcus are kneeling beside something in the grass, the rain soaking them straight to the bone. They don't even look at me as I rush up behind them, too taken with the state of—

"Oh my god," I gasp and throw myself onto my knees beside them.

Atlas is lying in the grass in a pool of golden liquid, smiling at his nest-mates in a way that makes my stomach drop. It looks like a goodbye, and I fucking refuse to let it be that.

I sweep my eyes over him, trying to take stock of what the hell happened. His arms are at his sides, and his body has been cut in half on a slant. That golden liquid is his blood, and the ground is saturated with it. It's all over Marcus and Julius and Darius, who all look so lost and shaken. That look etched into Darius' features is what strikes me the most. He has never allowed himself to look uncertain before.

"Don't touch him," Marcus says sharply, though the bite in his voice is pure fear rather than anger.

"I—" I bite back the urge to soothe him, to tell him I won't because something begins to squirm under my skin.

Lightning strikes a short distance away, and the crack of thunder resonates in my bones. Something about that and the steady drum of the rain on my skin slowly forces my mind to calm, and a meditative state takes over me.

It's like my magic comes to life inside me. It pulses through me like a second heartbeat I can feel as clearly as my own, and it's calling out to Atlas. He is my mate even if he doesn't want me, and I won't let him leave me.

My hands reach out of their own volition, moving to rest over his chest. Another crack of lightning calls to my magic, and finally, it breaks free.

White light explodes around us.

Explodes out of me.

A rush of pain and pleasure floods my body, making me cry out. My palms burn and ache like I've held them to a stovetop, but my body throbs as if someone has been edging me for hours. I'm pretty sure my eyeballs roll into the back of my head, but all I can see is that blazing light.

We're all blinded for one breath, two, three. I stop trying to count the moments that seem to drag on. Then, as if it had never been there, the light goes out like someone flipped a switch to turn it off.

Atlas' eyes are on me, his pupils blown out and lips parted. Where his chest has been cut through is now closed with a golden scar.

None of us speak as the rain pounds harder against us. I don't know what I did, but it was something, and it was enough. I jerk my hands back and rush to scramble back, but Atlas' hand shoots out, and he grabs me.

"Firefly," he murmurs, stroking his thumb back and forth on my hand as he clutches it. Like I'm the one in need of soothing.

I guess he can see it on my face before I feel it. The pain and pleasure fade so quickly that all my emotions and endorphins come crashing down on me. A broken sob tears out of my throat before I slap my free hand over my mouth to catch it. Tears roll down my face in thick, anime-like globs that mix with the fresh rain.

"Hush now, Firefly, I'm alright." His voice is soft and kind. Different from the sharp disdain he normally speaks to me with, and it makes me crumple over him.

My body folds like a wet piece of paper, and I shield him from the rain only to further soak him with my tears.

"We need to get them inside."

"To the nest. It will be best for his healing."

"Should we each take one?"

"I don't think she would let us separate them?"

I vaguely hear their voices, but my racked sobs and the pounding rain, in addition to my lack of giving a shit, keep me from placing who says what exactly. I tense on top of Atlas when they mention separating us.

Atlas draws my hands to his lips and presses soft kisses into my palm. "My Firefly, so bright and beautiful," he murmurs, his words sending a shiver down my spine.

A soft wash of clarity brushes over me as I cling to Atlas.

"Lift them together," Darius commands.

"We need to get them out of the rain before she gets sick," Julius adds.

"On three." Marcus cuts in.

I shut my eyes as they lift us. I clutch Atlas as if my life depends on it when really I think his life is more the one in question. Who knows what I did or if it will hold?

I can only hope.

CHAPTER 29

DARIUS

At some point during the laborious process of carrying them inside, Charlotte passed out. Something about the cold and the use of her magic took the wind right out of her.

Before going into the nest, Marcus takes Charlotte into his arms, and Julius orders Atlas to strip, which is only made harder as he refuses to let go of Charlotte's hand. When I try to pry her fingers from Atlas', I'm met with resistance on both sides. Charlotte's magic sends painful pinprick shocks through my hands, and Atlas nearly headbutts me just to get me to leave them be.

"Leave her in her clothes. It's not right to strip her now," Atlas says, his voice low and laced with a growl.

"She'll catch something if she stays in her wet clothes," Julius says, earning another growl from Atlas. "Marcus and I have seen her naked, so I think it's best we undress her and tuck her into the nest."

"I won't let my Firefly go," Atlas says adamantly, squeezing her hand.

It makes me both proud and exasperated to see him finally give in to his feelings for Charlotte, but the timing could not be worse.

"Atlas, let her go," I snap, sending a surge of my influence through our bonds and reinforcing it with magic.

The younger gargoyle grits his teeth, baring them all to me in a grimace as he slowly lets her go one finger at a time. Charlotte releases a sad little noise, shifting slightly in Marcus' arms before settling with her face pressed into his pec.

"I should push you down the damned stairs," he hisses, lunging toward me before stopping short.

I don't flinch and hold back the roll of my eyes at his posturing.

Marcus slowly edges around him and takes Charlotte into the nest. Julius follows quickly after him, snapping the door shut and sliding the lock into place with an audible *click*.

Atlas glares at me across the short landing, where we normally take off our shoes before we enter the nest. I let him have his broody moment before crossing my arms. It's time to be the alpha.

"Where did you go, Atlas?" I demand.

Now that he isn't bleeding out, I can play the bad alpha.

"It's none of your business," he snaps, crossing his arms over his chest to mock me.

The new golden scar on his dark skin is beautiful in the same way a banshee is.

Whatever was strong enough to nearly rip Atlas apart is a problem for all of us, and he knows that, but he's being a stubborn arsehole.

Atlas leans against the door to the nest, his wings tucked neatly behind him as he continues to glower. He is still the same head-strong youngling he was all those years ago, when he finally showed us who he is.

"It's all my business. I am your alpha, unless you've forgotten," I snipe.

Atlas scoffs. "As If I could forget with the chokehold you keep on our magic."

"To protect you—"

"From what? Being able to learn for ourselves how to control it? Are you so insecure that you keep the power born to you and forged into me held so tightly we can hardly draw on it?" His questions are laced with venom and sting me viciously.

"You are being hurtful on purpose. We will discuss that later," I growl. "Where did you go?"

"And what if I don't tell you? Will you punish me?" He snickers, tail whipping back and forth.

I know he's goading me. I'm strong enough not to rise and meet the anger as it swells in my chest.

"You are a fucking brat. I've only ever tried to help you," I grit out.

"Because you are a guardian, a savior. Helping the weak is what you do." Atlas shakes his head.

The expression on his face makes my gut sink. It's something like pity.

"I'm not weak anymore, and neither are Julius and Marcus. You need to get over your complex and come back down to earth. We are a team." He shoves an index finger into my chest.

My mouth drops open, words on the tip of my tongue, but nothing comes out.

He thinks I have a complex?

"You are our leader. I won't even fight you on that, Darius, but you need to understand that sometimes enough is enough and just drop it," Atlas snaps, whipping away from me and toward the door. He presses his palm flat to the door as if he could reach through and touch Charlotte.

"That was an eye-opening conversation," I mutter, rubbing my chest lightly. "but it's good to see you've had a change of heart about Charlotte."

CHAPTER 30

CHARLOTTE

My BODY FEELS heavy and light and loose all over. My joints buzz from unleashing my magic, but slowly, the sensation is beginning to calm.

I groan, turning my face into the softness below me. I didn't know I was capable of whatever that was, but it felt so good. Magic felt more than natural.

"We should put a blanket on her. She's covered in goose bumps," Julius murmurs from above me, gently combing his fingers through my hair.

"We need to towel her off a bit first." Marcus argues lightly before something soft runs over my bare breasts.

My back arches toward the sensation, my nipples growing tight with want.

"Are you awake, little witch?" Julius asks, mouth against the shell of my ear.

I moan as Marcus gently pinches one of my nipples with the towel.

"I think so," I say without opening my eyes.

My head is floaty, and if I open my eyes, I'm afraid I'll have a spell of vertigo. I know I'm lying down so I won't fall. Even so, it would be embarrassing to puke all over them and the blankets.

The nest. Something inside me sighs, content to be in their sacred space with them.

"You brought me to the nest." I wriggle around into the blankets and sheets strewn onto the mattress floor. "And I'm naked."

"You're soaking wet," Julius purrs. "And not in the way we like. I wanted to make sure you wouldn't get sick on us, especially after you saved Atlas' life."

"What kind of guardians would we be if we didn't save you?" Marcus asks. I can hear the grin in his voice. "And what kind of mates would we be if we didn't blow your mind as a thank-you?"

A hand slips down my body to the juncture between my plush thighs. "Is this alright?" Julius asks.

My eyes flutter open, and I quickly search the small space for Atlas, finding him bundled up in blankets against a far wall with all my plushies surrounding him. I ache to hold him, but I'm afraid I'll only cause more pain. The distraction my other mates offer is too good to refuse.

I let my eyes droop closed again before I lick my lips, nodding. "Please."

"Anything for you, little witch," Julius says before pressing kisses to the side of my neck, starting just under my ear and going all the way down to my breasts.

He slides his hand down along my soaked lower lips before parting them.

Marcus groans like he's taken a punch to a vital organ.

"Fuck me, hold her open, just like that," he growls, and I hear his clothes hit the sheets before the weight of his body makes me shift downward.

Julius' fingers hold me open dutifully, and I whimper at how exposed I feel. Exposed and hot as shit with Marcus just staring at my pussy. Who knew I had a thing for body worship?

"Can I spit on your clit?" His warm breath ghosts over my pussy, and I feel myself fucking leaking for him.

"Please!" I moan, my hips aching slightly, begging for something to just touch me.

"Thank you," he says before drawing back. He spits on my clit, and my whole body vibrates with pleasure. "Gods, you are so damn pretty, Char. I can't get enough of you."

"Our perfect mate," Julius adds, running his fingers over my labia in a tantalizing tease.

"Please tell me one of you is going to fuck me," I say desperately, my empty cunt clenching around nothing, the desire burning me up just like my magic had.

"Of course we are. Just need you to let us know what you want," Julius murmurs, taking a nipple into his mouth and giving it a hard suck.

The sounds of clothes being discarded in a mad dash make my lips curl into a small smile. I bask in a moment of unseeing bliss before I feel the head of a deliciously hard cock nudge at my entrance.

I risk it, opening one eye and glancing at Marcus as he angles his body over mine, holding himself up with one hand and guiding his cock inside me with the other. He takes his time, letting each delicious ridge along his shaft pop inside me rather than just going ham and thrusting in all at once.

I arch into him, grinding against each inch he gives me. Moaning his name softly, I open my eyes slowly, looking at both handsome gargoyles as they worship every inch of my body.

Marcus brings the hand not holding his cock to my hip, gripping me tightly as he grits his teeth.

"So fucking tight and perfect, Char, can't ever get enough."

"I'm yours, Marcus." I vow to him.

"And me?" Julius asks, pulling away from my hard nipple with a pop.

He blows on the hardened bud, ripping a little whine from me.

"Of course, you jerk face," I grumble and grab his hair, pulling his face so close the tips of our noses brush. He's buck naked except for his stupidly handsome gold wire glasses. "Do you even need those?" I ask, not giving him time to answer me before crushing my lips against his.

He meets my kiss with gusto, nipping and sucking on my lips as Marcus rocks his hips, fucking me with deep, slow thrusts.

"You feel so damn good," Marcus moans, picking up his speed.

Our obscene wet sounds fill the room, and Julius groans.

"I don't want to pressure you, but I would love to fuck you next," Julius purrs, skimming his hands up and down my sides.

He sits up, and my face is level with his groin. It's then that I notice he has a red gem embedded in his pubic area.

I tip my head as I take it in and reach out my hand. When I brush against it, a warm pulse of magic makes my fingertips buzzy. "Whoa, how did I not notice this before?"

"You were beholding all of my awesomeness and didn't notice a silly little gem. Don't get all distracted by his monster cock and dick jewelry," Marcus says with a breathy chuckle.

"It's not my fault she likes shiny things." Julius grins down at me and winks. "You will love it against your clit."

My mouth suddenly goes dry. Would it be weird to ask my gargoyle boyfriend to tap out so I can feel the magic gem of my other gargoyle boyfriend against my clit?

A groan sounds from the other side of the room. Marcus freezes mid-thrust, his eyes flicking toward Atlas. Marcus curses softly and in a language that I can't understand, but he doesn't clarify and just grinds into me. It's hot.

Julius sighs, standing slowly and giving me a view of said monster cock. It's huge, like 'my insides might come out' huge, and my pussy clenches in anticipation. The hussy knows she can take him even if my mind is hesitent.

"Fuck," Marcus groans. "You are not making it easy to hold back right now," he murmurs, leaning down and pressing kisses all over my face. "Is this tight pussy excited to swallow that cock?"

"More like terrified," I say with a nervous giggle. A blush burns my cheeks.

"We would never hurt you, Char. I would never let any of them hurt you." He strokes his fingers through my hair, fingernails sharpening slightly to run over my scalp.

"You're my favorite." I shoot him a teasing wink, but it doesn't stop him from beaming at me.

"Oh, fuck it," Marcus says as he grabs my left leg and lifts it onto his shoulder, letting his incredible dick slide even deeper into my pussy. "You deserve a good, hard fuck."

"Yes, please, I'm such a good girl," I moan, rutting against him, unable to help myself.

I have no clue where the whole "good girl" thing came from, but for now, it can stay.

"Yes, you are such a good girl," Marcus growls, and his pace is punishing in all the best ways.

"Atlas is awake, little witch. Are you alright with that?" Julius asks. "He needs to be in here to heal, but if you need us, we can move you to your room."

"No, if you're okay with it, then so am I." I force myself to lean up and settle on my elbow, glancing at Julius and Atlas across the room, staring at Marcus and me. "Please, let me stay. I need to be near you, Atlas. I need it."

I cry out as Marcus hits the perfect spot inside me. It lights me up from the inside out, and I swear I can feel the next crack of lightning in my veins.

"Of course, Firefly, I owe you a mountain of apologies," Atlas says with a sad smile as he and Julius walk on their knees back to Marcus and me.

He's naked when he finally reaches me, his bandages getting in his way. After quickly tossing them off, he kneels beside my head. His cock is incredible. It's studded along the shaft, with a deliciously wide head and balls that I would call beautiful. His coloring continues down his shaft like all of them, and I want to run my tongue along the white veins as if they were real veins.

"Apology accepted. Just please, please let me fuck you," I moan, reaching for him but waiting for him to make contact."

Atlas takes my hand and rests it on his thigh, so close to that heavy cock.

"I would be honored to be with you, mate." His soft rumble makes me laugh before I'm drowned by pleasure again.

"I'm going to come, Marcus," I gasp, my free hand shooting out and gripping his biceps.

"Come for me, baby. I want you to make every inch of this nest yours." He bares his teeth as he moves even faster, even harder.

His cock is bashing against my cervix in a perfect mix of pleasure and pain.

I lose it.

I come so damn hard I think I black out, or white out. The lightning outside splits the sky, each crack a wave of my pleasure.

"Gods, you are beautiful, Firefly," Atlas murmurs.

CHAPTER 31

ATLAS

I'VE ALWAYS KNOWN the best things in life happen slowly and all at once.

Falling for Charlotte is easier than breathing. I feel like a fool for letting my hang-ups keep me from her. This witch has changed my life irrevocably. I was going to die, and then there she was, pushing herself to the limits of her magic and weaving me back together.

As she comes apart under Marcus, a small bite of jealousy eats at me. I want to make her feel good, make up for all the shit I put her through. This is the first step of my penance, watching her fuck my nest-mates. Marcus grunts as his own orgasm makes his hips jerk, fucking his cum into her.

She writhes and pants as she comes down from her pleasure. Marcus withdraws, his cock still ready to please her, and his cum drips out of her. The pearlescent liquid makes her pussy even more beautiful somehow.

"Mind if I go next?" Julius asks in a soft voice.

He's kneeling beside me, his cock hard and jutting out straight in front of him, like it's locked on to our mate.

"I'm not the one you should be asking." I jerk my chin toward the blissed-out Charlotte.

"Yes, please, fuck me," she pants, tipping her eyes us both. "But remember, I can hear you both. Orgasms do not take away that one of my five senses."

Julius grins like he's won the lottery, and he shoves Marcus out of the way to take his place between her plush thighs. He strokes them, and I'm so jealous I could spit venom.

"I promise this is going to be incredible." The gargoyle adjusts his glasses, pushing them far up his nose. He takes his cock in hand and taps it against her clit three times before slowly sliding down and notching himself at her entrance.

For a split second, I see a shred of fear run through her before she nods.

"I'm ready."

CHARLOTTE

I was absolutely not ready. All of my gargoyles are big, huge even, but Julius...it's on another level. His length is so impressive that it makes me fear for my internal organs and my already bruised cervix. I took his dick before, but I'm so sensative I think I might pass out.

As he notches his head at my sopping entrance, I gasp. He's so fucking hot and hard. I have to bite into my cheek to keep from bucking and taking him into me before we're both ready.

The bite of fear makes me even wetter for him, and he uses the added slick to push the first of too many inches inside me.

"Fuck." The moan punches out of me. "Why do you have to

be smuggling a baseball bat in your pants? I just want to feel your gem." The words are almost a whine as I glance down.

The magical gem seems to wink at me as it catches the soft light in the room. I'm desperate to know what it feels like against my clit, against my pussy in any way, really. I just need it.

"Soon, little witch, soon," Julius purrs.

He slides one of his hands to my clit, two fingers circling the sensitive nub at a tantalizingly slow pace. Another inch sinks in, and the stretch is intense.

"Gods," he grunts. His abs flex, seeming so human in this moment of passion. "Are you sure you don't get tighter every time we fuck you?" He picks up his pace on my clit.

I cry out, hips jerking and taking more of his length in the process. My pussy becomes a waterfall around him as he works magic on my pussy.

"Good girl," Julius croons as he inches inside me.

Halfway in, I feel overstuffed. Three-quarters of the way inside, I feel him at my damn cervix. All the way in, I'm struggling to breathe, stuffed with so much cock. That gem finally presses into my clit. It's cooling for a second before the thing begins to *vibrate*.

I detonate. My second orgasm is just as intense as the first.

My hand on Atlas's thigh tightens, and he grunts, a gush of warm liquid splattering on my hand as I spasm. I jerk my hand to my face and lick up all the delicious pearly pre-cum that Atlas gave me.

"I'm going to move now," Julius says breathlessly.

"Show-off," Marcus grumbles, arms folded over his chest as he frowns.

He claimed the spot above my head, my brown hair tumbling over his pretty yellow skin, and he pulls my head into his lap. He strokes his fingers through my hair softly with one hand as the other goes to his cock.

Marcus strokes his ridged shaft tantalizingly slow, and my

mouth waters with the need to have one of them in it, but both he and Atlas are just out of reach.

"Hey," Julius chuckles. "I offered to install one for you too, but you were too scared."

"Install?" I croak.

"We can't exactly pierce," Atlas says, shaking his head and grinning as his cock kicks again, eager for more of my attention. "So that crazy bastard installs each of those shiny things into his body." He gestures to the jewelry pressed to my clit and then up to Julius' studded horns.

Reds and blues and yellows shine with each tilt of his head. He put each one in himself. I don't know whether to be impressed, horny, or afraid of how much punishment he can handle.

"OK, enough talk." I wave my hands in the air. "I need to be pounded into the nest, please and thanks."

"Your wish is my command, Charlotte."

CHAPTER 32

DARIUS

I SHOULDN'T BE LISTENING, but I can't help myself. Charlotte's cries of ecstasy as my nest-mates take turns with her are the finest music. Each sigh, whimper, moan, and scream is another instrument in the symphony of her pleasure. I'm addicted to each sound.

I want to be in there, in our nest, helping to please her, but I've been a horrible leader. I've done everything I promised myself I wouldn't do: control their power, keep them from wielding it, making them feel small. I'm just like my father.

The thought is a bitter pill.

"Julius!" Charlotte cries, and I shiver.

I can't help but want to know what she would sound like crying out my name. I'm a selfish leader, and that needs to change. Immediately. For the good of this nest, my nest, *our* nest.

CHARLOTTE

Julius wrings another three orgasms out of me before filling me with his own release.

I tap Atlas' thigh and croak, "Mercy, please, mercy."

The green gargoyle above me chuckles as he slowly withdraws every inch of that anaconda from my oversensitive pussy. A flood of our combined cum gushes out of me when he finally pulls free.

"Can't handle us, mate?" Julius asks with a grin.

Atlas snorts, and Marcus grins like a fool. I pout.

"I very much can handle you all, just one at a time, preferably with a fifteen-minute break in between," I huff.

Atlas chuckles as he leans down, pressing a soft kiss to my forehead. "Then you will have the rest of the night off. My fist has satisfied me for many years. I can handle one more night."

"Nuh-uh!" I argue, rolling over and practically tossing myself into his lap. "No way, you deserve a little something for not being such an asshole, in my humble opinion."

"You honor me, Firefly," Atlas says with a satisfied purr. "I'll take whatever you want to give me."

I purse my lips before I grin and lean down to give his cock head a kiss. The dark stone streaked with white and gray veins is so damn alien and hot. I was never one to be too adventurous, but when in Ireland.

"I want to take you in my mouth," I murmur, pressing hot kisses up and down his shaft.

His texture is by far the most addictive that I've encountered with my gargoyles. The bumps that run along his shaft are akin to small spherical subdermal piercings. I've never been with anyone who had any dick jewelry, and now I'm with four men who are all decked out.

"How did we get so lucky?" Julius muses from his resting position beside me. He strokes his hand up and down my back, his fingers tracing my spine. "Such a cock-hungry mate we have."

"Well, it's because we're the best protectors," Marcus says, as if the answer is completely obvious.

"Maybe we saved some lesser God, and they granted us this delightful firefly as a boon," Atlas whispers right before gasping.

His head slides between my lips, and I waste no time sucking in my cheeks. I want to blow his mind, show him how good I am for all of them.

Even if I forgive him for being an asshole before, I still want to give him pause for giving me such a hard time. It's only fair.

I pull off his cock with a pop. "When did you come up with that little nickname?" I ask, arching a brow at him, my hand taking over for my mouth and stroking up and down.

Atlas makes a bit of a face, and Julius barks a laugh.

"You are not going to like where it came from," Atlas grumbles, bucking his hips slightly and fucking my fist.

"Try me." I urge him.

"He used to call you a pest." Julius snickers.

"A firefly isn't a pest. Were you really just being that much of a brat?" I ask, heat rising to my cheeks and absolutely lighting me up.

He gives me a grin that would melt the panties off me if I wasn't already naked.

"Oh, fuck you." I smirk, rolling my tongue over the head of his cock in teasing figure eights.

Atlas groans, his delicious salty pre-cum flooding my mouth.

"I'm sorry, I didn't mean for it to be so...harsh. I was fighting my attraction to you. You burned me up from the inside out, and now I know why. I just had to give in to you, and it would be—" He cries out as I take him to the hilt.

I growl softly around his cock, the vibrations making him shiver as I suck his cock like it's my job. I move my hand that had been working his shaft down to those pretty balls, and I fondle them. It's a mind fuck to see and feel them as stone for all of a breath before they melt and become as soft as flesh. It's such a trip.

"Gods, she's going to suck my soul out," Atlas chokes out.

"Oh yeah, she's really good with her mouth. Best I have ever had," Marcus purrs, and I growl again.

Marcus and Julius shift away from Atlas and me, giving us space to explore one another as they watch. My green gargoyle pulls the other man into his lap so they face each other, stroking both of their cocks in his fist.

The thought of them with anyone else burns my blood in a way that makes me want to get vengeance. It's more than a little irrational. I was with people before, and I am nowhere near as old as any of them. Of course, they've fucked people before me, but they don't have to talk about it while I'm bare-ass naked and dripping with their cum.

"She did not like that," Atlas says, sliding a hand into my hair and gently pulling me off him. "We've had others, but none will compare to you. You're the one we were all born and made for."

I flush and press a kiss to his inner thigh. "Fair. I've had sex with other people too."

Julius grunts and Marcus curses.

"We know, and we are glad there were men before us to prepare your perfect pussy for our cocks," Julius says, though he runs his nails gently down my back.

The bite of pain makes me tingle all over, and I shiver, my pussy suddenly hungry once again for cock.

"OK, I think I'm recharged for you, Atlas." I sit up slowly, trying to ignore the gush of fluids from my pussy as I eye him up and down.

When it comes to fucking these guys, I'm suddenly insatiable.

Atlas leans back, spreading his knees and showing off his body. "I'm yours. Take me, Charlotte."

I don't need to be told twice. I dive onto him, tackling him to the bed. I giggle as his hair falls into his face, obscuring his eyes before he pushes it back.

"Are you okay with me riding you?" I ask as I angle my hips over his, lining his cock up with my entrance.

"I'm yours," Atlas breathes, his eyes holding mine and finally showing me the passion beneath his granite surface.

I sink onto his cock in a single motion, crying out from the intensity. Each nodule rubs my inner walls in ways that make it impossible to keep the mewls and moans in.

Atlas grips my hips, helping me rise and fall onto his cock, taking it from root to tip.

"Right there, right there," I gasp, biting into my lip as the pleasure mounts.

I feel it in the atmosphere before I feel it inside me.

Cracking, booming, expanding, shattered. It all hits me at once.

My pussy spasms around Atlas' cock, gushing as he keeps my hips moving, the pleasure of my orgasm stealing my breath.

Atlas continues to move me but begins to pump his hips upward, prolonging my orgasm before his own crests. He cries out my name as he fills me with thick, hot cum.

CHAPTER 33

CHARLOTTE

WE HAVE three days of relative peace before Eloise comes knocking with an enormous book that seems to be bound in human leather. Julius, Marcus, and Atlas, who have become planets orbiting around me, lead us into the sitting room with promises of snacks and space so that we can talk.

Eloise gives Atlas, in particular, a strange look as he leaves us alone.

"That one has always been a lot to handle. It's good to see you've taken him in hand."

I sputter at Eloise's choice of words and give her a "what did you just say" look, to which she replies with a shrug.

"I've found something I think is interesting. These are records of magic users born on the Isles from the eighteenth century forward. I believe I've found your parents," she says, opening the book.

My stomach sinks.

"My parents weren't that old when they passed or when they

had me." I fiddle with my fingers. I've gotten a little better with the biting, but the urge still hits hard when stress mounts.

"Witches don't age in the same ways that mortals do. We are not immortal creatures, but we can come damn close if we have potent enough lineage." She lays the book on a small side table that groans under the weight of the tome. "I've found the marriage record of one Collum Ryan and Gwyneth Hawthorn. Your parents had similar names, if I'm not wrong."

"Cal Ryan and Gwen Ryan." I bite my lip, a flush of annoyance rising up and making my cheeks pink. I feel like an idiot.

"I knew it." Eloise tuts, pointing to the crossing of two heavy red lines on a twisted tree that seems to span many pages. "It was a grand marriage, quite the thing back in the day. I didn't bother to attend. Other shit needed to get done, but it was a big to-do," she says with a dismissive wave of her hand.

"So my parents were hundreds of years old when they had me?" I blanch.

"Apparently so. There is little record after the marriage, but I don't see it as out of the realm of possibility for them to move to America and birth a child. Seems par for the course for those of the old blood, planting roots on new lands and all."

I wilt back into my seat, a groan slipping out of my lips with my heavy exhale.

"Not what I expected," I admit.

"With the powers you seem to possess, it seems like just the thing." Eloise nods, looking over me appraisingly. "And it seems you have strong mates. They will be a good temper to your magic."

"I'm really...confused." I let out a shaky laugh.

"Don't be, Charlotte. You have your entire life to look through this damned book if you'd like. It's of no use to me anymore." She pats the heavy cream pages of the strange book. "It will be of much more use to you, seeing as I don't have powers to control the weather."

"I can't really control the weather," I grumble.

"Those lightning hearts in the sky some days back weren't you?" Eloise crosses her arms over her chest, smirking at me.

My face burns instantly, the tips of my ears growing hot in the same breath. "I didn't do it on purpose."

"Even so"—she gestures to the book—"this will help you learn, and you can always come and ask us old witches questions, but this is all on the lot of you now."

The door creaks open slowly, and I whip my head toward it to see who is coming in. I'm startled to see the one gargoyle who has been actively avoiding all of us far more successfully than I would like to admit.

"Darius." I shoot out of my seat and rush over to him. I grab one of his hands, hoping that if I have hold of him, he won't run. "We need to talk."

Darius glances past me into the room at Eloise. He gives her a small nod of acknowledgment before meeting my eyes. He looks paler than normal, and my stomach twists in knots. His expression is not impassive in the slightest. He looks sick at the prospect of speaking with me.

"What can I help you with, Charlotte?" he asks, voice all calm, cool, and collected.

Behind us, Eloise rises and leaves the sitting room through a small side door, leaving me alone with my alpha mate.

"Eloise told me a bit about my parents. Apparently they were old too." I laugh, the sound once again mildly hysterical. "And they had a lot of power, and my mates are supposed to help me temper the power."

He stiffens at the words but pulls me deeper into the room, sitting me in the same tall wingback chair I've since learned he prefers. He doesn't speak again until he has tucked me in with a blanket Julius made for me.

"I can't."

"Why can't you?"

"I'm not a good alpha." His voice goes soft, eyes turning glassy.

"I've abused my powers as the alpha and made my nest-mates distrust me. I won't allow the same thing to happen with you." He takes both of my hands and kisses each of my knuckles. "My sweet mate, I won't ever have you believe I've taken advantage of you."

My mouth flaps open and closed, unable to form words as my mind races. I repeat his words over and over in my head. I can see it, just the barest bit, and he's being way too shitty to himself.

"Stop that," I finally say.

"Stop?" Darius asks, sinking to his knees beside my chair, still holding my hands reverently. "I'm doing this for you, for *us*."

"No, I don't think you are. You're running away because someone pointed out a mistake you made," I say, shocked by my brazenness. "Have you tried apologizing? Showing them it won't happen again?"

Darius pauses, shifting his eyes down to my hands. He grazes his fingertips over each of my fingers as he mulls over what I said.

I huff out a breath, trying to loosen some of the tension in the room.

"You are so wise, little mate," Darius chuckles, pressing delicate and sensual kisses against my fingers.

I can't help but get a little hot under the collar of my new sweater. Julius made it for me, and the green is the same as his stone form. I've been wearing it any chance I get, but it's not the most breathable piece of clothing I own. I tug at the neck, blushing deeply.

"I wish, I'm just...Charlotte."

"Charlotte, Charlotte Ryan. Beautiful witch, excellent painter, with a beautiful heart and a clever mind," he whispers, gazing up at me with lust pooling in his dark eyes.

My center instantly grows wet, soaking my underwear and possibly the crotch of my overalls.

"I have to say, I've had all my mate's cocks, but not yours. My alpha has been staying away." I tease him gently, pulling him closer by our joined hands.

He chuckles, breath shaking as his eyes rove hungrily over me all tucked up in his chair. "I've been wallowing in self-pity, I suppose. How can I ever make you forgive me?"

I pause and purse my lips, making a brief show of slipping one hand from his and tapping my index finger against my chin. "I think if you dick me down, then I'll think about forgiving you."

Darius' eyes shine, and he grins at me, showing off more teeth than is polite. "Anything for my mate."

In one swift move, Darius takes me into his arms, throws the blanket that was wrapped around me into a far corner, and shuts the book that Eloise had left open, pushing the table far away from us. I gasp and clutch his neat dress shirt, ruining the perfect press of it with my sweaty hands. Surprising me further, Darius takes a seat in his favorite chair and sits me on his lap, facing him.

"I think this is going to be fun." He undoes the straps of my overalls with deft fingers and tugs them down to my waist. He lifts my sweater and T-shirt before ogling my breasts clad in a lace bra.

I've upped my game a bit at Kennedy's recommendation. Now that someone actually looks at my underwear, I want to make it worth looking at. Kennedy nearly burst my eardrum when I told her about my mates before giving me a variety of websites that ship to the middle of nowhere in Ireland.

"Perfection in the flesh," he breathes, pulling me close and kissing the daylights out of me.

His mouth is so hungry on mine that it takes a heartbeat for my mind to catch up. His desire melts me. I press against him, wanting every inch of him against me, inside me.

I groan.

"So needy." He tuts, lifting me easily with one hand and jerking my overalls clean off my body.

My mouth pops open, forming a surprised *O*.

"Let me give you something, then."

His dark promise makes me shiver and then moan as he lifts

me all the way up so my pussy is level with his face. His tongue lashes across my sensitive flesh through the matching lace.

"Fuck!" I yelp, gripping the back of the high chair, nearly lurching forward and tossing myself over it.

His mouth doesn't let up. He sucks on my lower lips, tonguing my clit roughly and making me wish I knew a spell to make the rest of my clothes vanish.

"Tastes like mana, the most heavenly dew," he purrs against my clit, pulling another moan from me.

"Please don't call it dew. I'll take so many other words, but dew makes me feel like a leaf or something," I pant, my brain cells trying desperately to get to work.

Darius chuckles and draws back from my pussy, glancing up at me. His mouth is wet with my juices, and his scruff glistens. Something possessive inside me roars in triumph.

My mate has my pussy juices all over his face, as he should.

"I didn't mean to offend you." He presses kisses to the insides of my thighs. "As distracted as you are, I think I'm doubly so." He growls softly and drops me into his lap.

His hard cock jabs me in the ass immediately. He's thicker than any of my other gargoyles, with a length that falls somewhere in the middle of the nest's impressive endowments.

I lick my lips and grind against his slacks, leaving a huge wet spot as I leak all over him.

He grips my ass, rocking my hips over his length. His eyes lock onto the spot where we're almost connected and shine brighter. His horns seem to lengthen, and his wing tips sharpen into claw-like hooks, his face taking on sharper and more monstrous angles.

He's still hot as sin but much more gargoyle than before.

"Whoa," I moan.

"You make me want to lose all my control. You are everything," Darius growls, tearing my panties away with a flick of his lengthened claws.

He jerks his zipper down and frees his impressive cock.

I have one second to gape at the twisting pattern that makes up the shaft of his cock before he plunges inside me. My eyes roll to the back of my head, and a desperate, wanting moan punches out of me.

My alpha pounds into me from below, owning my pussy with his monstrous cock. His claws dig into the flesh of my ass, and the prick of pain makes my skin break out in goose bumps.

"Yes, Darius, so good," I cry, trying to move my hips with him, to ride his cock as much as he's fucking into me.

"My mate, my delicious little witch." He nips at my collarbones, canine teeth sharp and pricking at my tender skin.

"Yours, I belong to your nest," I gasp, knowing what words really set my gargoyles off now.

Darius grunts, fucking me harder, his cock swelling with his approaching climax.

I slip my hand between our bodies and rub my clit harshly, trying to build myself up faster. My breaths come out in ragged pants as my alpha uses me so well.

"You may belong to the nest, but it's my cum as the alpha that will let our magic claim you as our mate," he purrs, the darkness of his tone only making the words sexier.

"Please, harder. Darius, fuck me harder," I beg, my hand finding the perfect tempo to match his pounding.

He bares his sharp teeth at me, eyes flashing, and my whole body tingles as he uses magic to fuck me faster and harder.

I explode on his cock, and the scream that tears out of me rattles the windows of the castle. My magic lashes out and is met by him, *them*. Their magic tangles around mine like cords.

CHAPTER 34

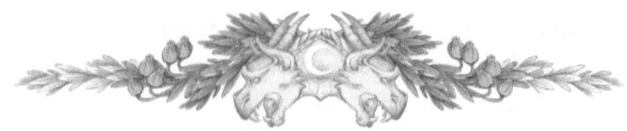

ATLAS

I feel the tug before my nest-mates. The pull of immense magic leading back to our alpha.

I snort, rubbing my chest over where our connection lays, giving Julius and Marcus a look before darting off. If anyone is going to deal with this properly, it's me. Finding Darius fucking our mate is not where I first imagined he would be. I freeze in the doorway, watching them as the magic fizzles out, loosening its hold on our bonds.

"Really? Needed a boost, did you, old man?" The words are out of my mouth before I can think.

Darius is up in a flash, his cock just tucked into his slacks and Charlotte left panting on his chair, pearlescent cum dripping down the insides of her thighs and onto the leather of the seat.

"Atlas," he growls, his features twisted up from the use of the magic to herald us.

He's more gargoyle than we normally are in our resting states, so I rise to meet him, pulling on my magic to grow just that much taller, my features becoming more monstrous.

"Darius," I deadpan, flicking out a hand to inspect my black claws.

"You haven't taken this form in a long time." His eyes widen, and he slowly releases more of the magic, shrinking just slightly and becoming softer. Well, as soft as a creature made of stone can be.

"I've finally gotten more of my magic back," I bite back, shifting back to my more human state.

Charlotte is staring at us, her chest rising and falling fast.

"You guys are such jerks to each other. I hope you know that," she says before closing her eyes to catch her breath.

"I know I'm a jerk," Darius says, drawing my attention back to him.

I arch a dark brow, crossing my arms tightly over my chest. "Finally admitting it."

"Yes," Darius grits out, frowning. "I have been an asshole, and I'm sorry."

I blink at my nest's alpha, taking him in for the first time in days. He looks smaller somehow, defeated or weighed down by something.

"You"—I inhale sharply—"apologize?"

"Yes, I've made a lot of mistakes." Darius runs a hand through his hair, sinking further away from his gargoyle form and taking on the warm brown skin tone he favors, his hair going dark brown and soft, his stubble changing to match. "I want to be a better leader, someone more deserving of the title 'alpha.'"

"It's about time," Julius says suddenly. He rests a hand on my shoulder from behind. "I love you, Darius, but you were so afraid of becoming your father that you did it in a roundabout way."

"Gargoyle daddy has daddy issues?" Charlotte asks with a soft smile on her lips, eyes still closed peacefully.

"I am not a daddy," Darius chokes out.

"Yes, you are," Marcus singsongs, coming into the sitting room from the small offset room. "You're the daddy, and Julius is the mommy. I'm the loveable, sexy uncle, and Atlas is the moody teenager."

"Fuck you." I scoff, trying to suppress my laugh.

Charlotte gives us no such kindness. She giggles incessantly.

"Charlotte opened my eyes." Darius looks back at her like she hung the moon in the sky. "And I want to work with you all to make this nest better."

"Oh, so she opened your eyes? Don't you mean she made you cum so hard you want to be a better gargoyle?" Marcus asks, sliding over and tossing his arm around Darius' shoulder. "Don't worry, D, we've all been there."

CHARLOTTE

"I am not holding out on you, Kennedy," I laugh as she squeaks in indignation through the phone.

It's later in the day, and I'm blessedly alone, so I can talk to my sister.

"You so are! You can't just not tell me about the details of their very nonhuman monster dicks!" she cries.

"Well, you're just going to have to get some fancy monster dick for yourself." I tease her, and she goes eerily silent on the other end. "Something you want to tell me?"

"No!" she snaps too quickly.

I narrow my eyes at the ceiling and blow a raspberry at her through the phone. "Fine, don't tell me," I sniff. "You could ask me a little something more appropriate, like what gift they basically proposed to me with."

For a beat, my sister is dead silent. The line crackles with the intensity of her shock before she asks, "What gift did they basically propose to you with?"

"It's the heart of the nest," I say in awe, thinking of the beautiful stone that has little bits of all of them in it. I have it tucked away for safekeeping. It's more than just some rock with an uncanny resemblance. It has actual power in it. "It's basically the most beautiful rock I've ever seen."

I can hear the smile on Kennedy's face. "Of course you would get excited about being gifted a rock."

"Isn't that all diamonds are? Rocks." My brow arches at her, even if she can't see it.

"Yes, but they're shiny rocks." She snickers softly.

"My rock is the shiniest! The best rock that there is, diamonds can get bent," I growl.

My curtains flap as some of my magic rises to defend my mates from the slight. The lights in the room flicker and pop momentarily.

Kennedy laughs at me across the line, jarring me out of my little tantrum.

That slight use of magic alerts my mates, and my door creaks open. My mates stand in the doorway, their eyes asking a million silent questions that distract me from my sister hanging up on me.

Julius is the first to step into my room and join me on my bed. "Everything alright?"

"Kennedy was making fun of the nest's heart." I pout, feeling stupid that I pulled on our shared magic because I got a little upset, more defensive than upset, really.

Being a witch is hard when you're in training. What I wouldn't give for a full-on training montage.

Marcus joins us on the bed, taking my legs and laying them across his lap. Atlas follows and sits beside my head, lifting it softly and sliding his lap under it, making for a wonderful pillow. Julius takes a seat beside Marcus and takes one foot into his lap. He presses his thumb into my arch, and I fight a groan. Darius joins us last, sitting beside me and resting his hand on my hip, making me feel safe and grounded.

"We'll have to invite her to visit so she can see how sickly in love with you we are," Atlas says with a vicious grin.

"*Or* we could visit New York." I grin back at him.

EPILOGUE

ATLAS

THREE MONTHS LATER.

"My dick is starting to hurt." Marcus complains, flexing said aching appendage, which he insists needs to be hard in order to be captured perfectly.

With both arms behind his head, he poses against the wall, appearing relaxed, while his cock remains rock hard in front of him.

Charming.

"I told you being flaccid works just fine when it comes to long paintings," Charlotte says with a little giggle behind her massive canvas.

Her pretty brown eyes flash for a moment over the top edge of the canvas before she artfully slashes her paintbrush across the canvas.

"I hate to agree with Marcus, but I'm cramping," Julius grumbles, his own pose the contrapposto.

I snort from my seated position across from Darius. Having the only working brain cells in this nest, we chose to be seated for

225

the portrait. Even if our little Firefly talked us into being naked, we wanted to be comfortable at least. I arranged the chessboard so that I could put our alpha in check. If we are going to be captured in all our glory, then I need a truly significant moment immortalized.

"We don't cramp," Darius says dryly. He chose a very thinker-esque pose. "They just want more of your attention, little witch."

"I can't say I blame them," I huff.

My pose is rather boring, seated with one leg resting over the other, one hand resting gently on the table, and the other on my thigh. It's easy enough to hold as we go into the second straight hour of the painting.

"I'm almost done laying down the under colors. I want this to be perfect. It's going in the nest." She sounds exasperated.

"I'm pretty sure you could light a piece of toilet paper on fire, and Julius would let you frame it in the nest," I quip.

Julius gives me a withering glare but doesn't contradict me.

"Enough moving," Charlotte says, stepping out from around the canvas, smudges of paint all over her. "If you guys can stay still for five more minutes, I'll be done, and then you can go back to saving the world."

I groan at the prospect of going on a mission. We took a short honeymoon to give the bonds between the nest and Charlotte time to develop and grow strong, but now it's time for life to take over.

"Actually, I'm all good," Marcus calls, putting on a face of intense focus, keeping his muscles tight and his cock hard by sheer force of will.

"Me too." Julius gives a swift nod before going eerily still.

Charlotte laughs, putting her hand clutching her brush at her hip, a smear of paint added to her overalls as she shakes her head at us.

"It's not our fault we have the most enchanting mate at home." Darius tilts his head to the side to stare at her.

Our Firefly goes bright red, straight down her neck and to the tips of her ears.

"How about we call it a day?" she asks, setting down her brush and undoing one of the straps of her overalls, letting it fall to her side.

I'm on her the next moment, hands holding the sensual swells of her hips. I press a hard kiss to her mouth, devouring her lips before spinning her to face my nest-mates.

"Shall we show Firefly that she has become our world?" I purr against the column of her neck.

"I could not agree more." Darius rises from his seat, changing to his more monstrous form, something we've discovered that our little witch enjoys, and sweeps forward to capture her in his arms.

Charlotte screams in delight, bouncing and waving her hands in a way that signals for Julius and Marcus to join.

We fuck her until her voice grows hoarse and then fails her altogether.

It's the best painting session so far.

Acknowledgments

Thank you so much to all of my awesome author friends for taking a look at this silly little story for me! The inks to my editors, my cover designer and illustrator. I'm an artist but hot dang you guys are amazing! This book wouldn't be half of what it is without you, I can't express my gratitude enough.

One last thing; thank you! Yes, you reading this! Wow, you're a weirdo for reading this whole thing but I appreciate you so hard.

ABOUT THE AUTHOR

When Domina isn't creating spicy stories, they are probably indulging in the stories of others or finding other ways to escape the dullness of real life.

A lover of fantasy, omegaverse, and sci-fi, there isn't a day that goes by without another story idea bubbling up for her. You can expect novels, novellas, kindle-vella stories, LGBTQIA+ elements and hopefully swoon-worthy RH/heros/heroines!

www.ingramcontent.com/pod-product-compliance
Lightning Source LLC
Chambersburg PA
CBHW022112240626
47153CB00007B/2336